EYE OF THE STORM

BOOK ONE OF THE STORM CYCLE

R.K. KING

Stormwalker
MEDIA

Copyright © 2017 by R.K. King. All rights reserved.

No part of this publication may be reproduced, stored, or transmitted in any form or by any means, electronic, mechanical, photocopying, recording, scanning, or otherwise, without written permission from the publisher or author. It is illegal to copy this book, post it to a website, or distribute it by any other means without permission, unless for the use of passages or quotes used for incidental purposes such as reviews or critiques of said publication.

This novel is entirely a work of fiction. The names, characters, and incidents portrayed in it are the work of the author's imagination. Any resemblance to actual persons, living or dead, events, or localities is entirely coincidental.

All brand and product names used in this book are trademarked by their respective owners. Publisher and author are not associated with any product mentioned in this book. No companies or brands mentioned have endorsed this book.

ebook Edition ISBN: 9781393521709

Print Edition ISBN: 978-0995896536

Cover art by J Caleb Design - www.jcalebdesign.com

PRAISE FOR EYE OF THE STORM

Inventive and intriguing...

– BOOKVIRAL

"Dune meets Mad Max!"

– AMAZON REVIEWS

"What might be our future..."

– GOODREADS REVIEWS

*To Mom, for inspiring.
To Britney, for believing.
At last, I did it.*

*THERE ARE MANY WORLDS. LET US
SEE THEM ALL.*

Join the RK King Readers' Tribe and receive a FREE short story, as well as take part in occasional giveaways, updates, behind-the-scenes info, and much more! Join today at www.rkkingwrites.com

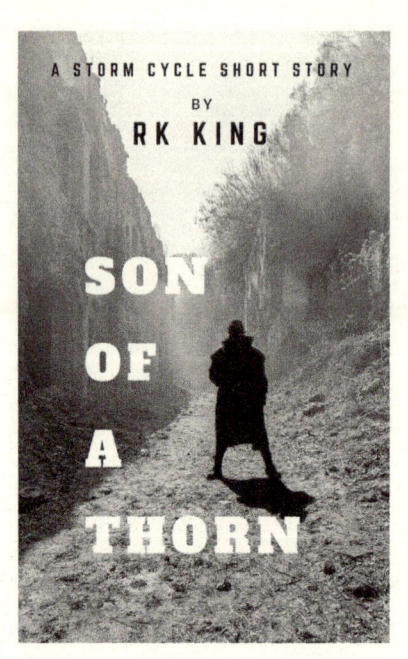

Son Of A Thorn is a short story prequel to Eye Of The Storm and The Storm Cycle. Receive it FREE by joining up with the RK King Readers' Tribe

CHAPTER 1

The strange vehicle sped across the desert sands as its driver, Deacon, raced for his life.

The vehicle was a motley collection of parts, pieced together from many types of cars; a side panel from an Oldsmobile, a hood from a Camaro, a back cab from an old Ford pickup. Though they somehow fit, they looked like they could also fall apart at any moment. In the back of the truck was a modified miniature garden, a mobile vegetable patch with vines hanging on wires and plants sprouting from the dirt laid inside.

Despite being barely able to see ahead in the swirling dust storm that surrounded him, Deacon pressed his foot on the gas as hard as he could as he glanced in the rear-view mirror. In the far distance stood the Storm Wall, the perceived border between the safety of the Eye and the raging chaos of the world beyond. The Storm Wall itself was massive, reaching well into the clouds and encompassing all that wasn't the Eye itself.

The Storm Wall crawled along at a deceptive pace, and Deacon knew his tribe, the Pathfinders, would have to move again soon.

Deacon reflected on the face looking back at him in the mirror; middle-aged and worn. Sandy hair, caked with the ever-present sand of the world around him, whipped in the high-velocity winds. A hard life peered from his eyes.

Deacon's moment of reflection broke as the mirror showed two vehicles similar to his, cobbled together in haphazard ways, following behind. Deacon sighed in relief, having thought those friends lost to the elements earlier. Perhaps they'd all make it after all.

Deacon glanced at his passenger, Creed. Creed was a little younger than Deacon, yet still sported that same weathered look. He had a bandolier of ammo wrapped around his torso and curved kukri blade sheathed in his belt. The man glanced in his side mirror. "Deacon, we got company!"

Deacon pressed the gas again. "Well, don't just sit there! How many?"

"Just one," Creed answered. "But it's a monster!"

Looking in his rear-view mirror, Deacon spotted a third vehicle that had joined them.

It was a much larger truck, adorned with spikes, hooks and barbs on the front and sides. It gave the appearance of a mechanical predator, shooting its way through the sandy sea toward its prey.

"Dogs!" Creed yelled.

The driver of the Dog truck was not alone. Two other Dogs were in the back, standing and leering over the truck's cab. They all had many piercings and tattoos that covered their faces and arms, and they hooted and hollered as they gained upon their target.

Creed drew his gun, an old and scraped pistol, and cocked it.

In the Dog truck, the two passengers aimed their weapons, improvised crossbows that fired metal junk shards, at one of the two Pathfinder vehicles in front of them. They opened fire, and sharp pieces of metal and scrap flew like angry hornets toward the third car. The metal pieces pierced the vehicle's shell with ease, cutting through the driver in a hail of shredding action.

The driver died instantly, and the car twisted and slipped into the dunes until finally flipping and smashing in a mangled heap.

"No!" Deacon screamed.

"Keep her steady," Creed said as he leaned out his window. Taking a moment to aim, he pulled the trigger and the Dog truck's front left tire blew. The truck skidded but did not falter, so Creed fired again. The other front tire exploded, and the truck came to a frantic halt.

A relief filled Deacon until a moment later fear overtook everything.

Another Dog truck appeared from a side trail. As it joined the chase, Deacon could make out three Dogs riding in the back cab. They almost instantly caught up to the other Pathfinder car. The Dogs then rummaged through their ordinance, pulling out a bottle of fuel. Stuffing a rag partly into the bottle, they then lit it on fire. One Dog raised it high to throw.

Creed fired his gun again, but his aim was off.

The bottle struck the back of the Pathfinder car, and an instant later, flames consumed it.

Deacon held back tears meant for his fallen comrades. He knew the Dogs would be on him in moments. Without thought he reached into his tunic and withdrew a small jade ring which had a chain looped around his neck. The ring itself had no fancy jewel inlays or even any intricate carving. Just a simple, smooth surface of jade.

As he caressed the surface of the ring between his fingers, he thought back to the day before when they'd left the tribe for this supply run.

If only he'd brought more help. If only he'd been a better leader. If only he'd properly said goodbye to his son...

Deacon got pulled from his thoughts as the Dog truck pulled up next to Deacon's side with ease. Drawn by the Dog's maniacal laughter, Deacon glanced out his window to look down the end of a crossbow.

This is it then, Deacon realized. *I'm sorry, Aiden...*

"Down!" Creed yelled, and Deacon followed the order without thinking. The Dog wielding the crossbow tried to track Deacon's movement, but froze as he faced Creed's pistol. Creed fired. The Dog fell from the back cab, his lifeless body crushed beneath the constantly racing tires of both vehicles.

Deacon twisted the wheel, and their car spun in the sand. He attempted a sharp u-turn, but the Dog truck kept pace with him and the remaining two Dogs in the back cab opened fire again.

Their shots went wide, piercing holes along the Pathfinder car's side. Creed jumped as a bullet made its way in and slipped just in front of his face, piercing out Deacon's window.

"That's it!" Creed growled. "Gimme your gun!"

Deacon did so, and Creed then shimmied out his window, half dangling off the side of their vehicle. The Dog truck made its way upon them again just as Creed hoisted himself horizontally, a gun wielded in each hand. He returned fire upon the enemy.

Both Dogs toppled out of the truck. That left just the driver. Creed howled in triumph.

But then the Dog truck slowed, and Deacon dared to look forward once more.

Ahead, Deacon saw his caravan approaching. A pair of armored trucks, accompanied by a handful of dirt bikes and dune buggies, bore down on the scene. The remaining Dog driver tried to wheel the truck around and escape, but Deacon's allies soon swarmed it and pulled the Dog from his seat. They forced the Dog to his knees just as Deacon emerged from his car.

Deacon approached the Dog, placing the jade ring back beneath his tunic. The driver was furious and strong, and the Pathfinders holding him struggled. Deacon stared at the Dog for a moment, knowing how much destruction men like this one brought upon his people.

"What do you think you're doing?" Deacon asked the kneeling Dog. "You have any idea how few of us are left?!"

The Dog chuckled. "Let me loose," he said. "I'll show you how to survive!"

Deacon glanced at the Dog truck, pointing at it. "This is ours now!"

The Dog glared. "Over my dead body!"

Only the tiniest eye twitch betrayed Deacon's calm reply. "All right."

Deacon walked to a nearby buggy and rummaged for a moment, then pulled away, wielding a large lead pipe. He returned to the Dog, gripping the pipe tightly. As he stood before the kneeling Dog, Deacon remained silent. Then he raised the pipe above his head, and when it came striking down, he took no notice of the wincing from his fellow Pathfinders.

The Dog gave out only one painful yelp before he became silent for good.

Eventually Deacon dropped the pipe. It thudded upon the desert ground, leaving caked blood to clump in the sand. He stared at the lifeless form before him for a minute, then turned and headed for his car. His fellow Pathfinders stood around him, but he did not direct his eyes to any of them.

"Take care of it," Deacon spoke softly as he passed Creed. Then, as he neared his car, he paused when he saw an approaching vehicle. As the vehicle came to a stop, Deacon recognized the figures who emerged from within.

Isaiah, a middle-aged man with a dark complexion, hopped out of the car and veered around to the passenger door. He opened it, allowing his passenger, Jonah, to exit.

Jonah was much older than Isaiah or Deacon. Wrinkles lines his worn face that seemed to go on forever, and his long white beard whipped behind him in the breeze. His failing eyes were soft as they homed in on Deacon.

"Thank you Isaiah," the old man spoke as he stepped out of the vehicle. He brought with him a tarnished metal cane, its surface dented and beaten through the years. He leaned upon it as soon as he was on his feet.

"Jonah. Isaiah," Deacon greeted them both.

"Deacon," Jonah said as he approached and hugged him. "I'm sorry we weren't here sooner. Isaiah can't drive worth shit."

"Didn't wanna give you a heart attack, old man," Isaiah scoffed.

"You got here when you could," Deacon replied.

Jonah noted the grisly scene behind Deacon, but didn't speak of it. "How many of ours?"

Deacon shook his head. Casualties meant lost supplies, and even worse, some mournful families he'd have to give the bad news to.

"Were you able to save your cargo?" Jonah asked.

"Mine, yes," Deacon said. "There'll be enough. At least for tonight."

"Good. We'll prepare the food right away," Jonah turned to the other Pathfinders. "Help my son with this!"

As people hurried to obey, Deacon glanced around. A look of concern came over him. "And what about my son? Where's Aiden?"

Jonah smirked. "Where else?"

CHAPTER 2

Though conflict was the way of life, there was a place where the people of the Tribes could gather in peace. The market.

As nomadic as the tribes were, the market also moved with the Eye. Vehicles with displays and goods stocked upon them advertised what the people had found or fought for out in the wastelands. Tools, food, weapons and various other curiosities were all available for the right price. The vendors, hailing from the various tribes of the Eye, waited with anticipation for the next customers.

Amidst the market's activities, two young men wandered. Aiden was taller than his friend Hobbes, athletic, and seeming to lead with a half-step ahead of his friend. Hobbes was more wiry, his unruly hair a mop over his eyes. They both wore simple, pocketed and zippered garments, fashioned by hand for weathering the elements of the wasteland.

"Busy these days," Hobbes commented.

Aiden nodded, taking in the many sights.

Hobbes glanced at his friend. "Hey, Aiden. You hear me or what?"

After a moment, Aiden finally looked to his awkward friend.

"Ah, there he is," Hobbes continued. "As I was saying, it's busy here today."

"Well," Aiden replied, nodding to a nearby kiosk operated by a group of young ladies. "That's not such a bad thing, Hobbes."

Hobbes chuckled at that, giving a wink to the girls as they passed.

At the next kiosk, however, Aiden paused.

Arranged on a table was a collection of handmade dolls. Each doll wore small robes and bandages. Little discs of glass - improvised goggles for weathering the Storm beyond the Eye - hid or covered their eyes. Aiden took one doll in hand, turning it over to inspect it.

"We share this space," Aiden said to Hobbes. "We're trapped in the Eye, all of us. I guess this is how we deal with it."

Aiden placed the doll back down, smiling at the young doll-maker who was watching them, a partially made doll in her hands. She smiled back, though with caution.

"You mean distractions," Hobbes said as they continued. "Forgetting we live in a moving cage."

Up ahead, vendors were selling animals in various-sized cages of their own. Mainly birds of different species, sold for food and eggs.

Hobbes couldn't help noting the trapped animals. "The Eye is a cage, Aiden. Don't forget that."

Aiden rolled his eyes, looking away, only to halt his sights on a few kiosks across the way. They were being run entirely by young women. As they attended to their duties, selling fabrics and food, one girl caught Aiden's attention.

"Nothing wrong with a little distraction, my friend," Aiden grinned as he left Hobbes to approach the women. "And don't you forget that."

The young woman who'd caught Aiden's eye was making short work of vivisecting a pig. Aiden cringed slightly as she thrust with her knife, slicing through bone and cartilage.

"Something you're interested in?" the young lady asked as she noticed Aiden staring.

Aiden gulped. "Uh, yeah. Maybe. Name's Aiden." He attempted to whisk his hair out of the way but failed miserably.

"Larina." She smirked.

"Look," Aiden stammered. "Me and my friend are just browsing. But I think we'll stop by again late-"

"That'd be nice," Larina said. "Plenty to offer."

Hobbes sighed at his friend's attempts, then turned away as a loud voice nearby made itself heard. He could see a gathering of people, with a commanding voice emanating from the center. He approached.

Aiden, not knowing what else to say, checked for backup from his friend. But Hobbes had wandered off, and so Aiden gave a final awkward shrug to Larina before catching up. He didn't notice Larina grin as he left.

The group of people were congregating around a solitary figure. It was a man, wrapped in a flowing purple robe with golden symbols embroidered upon it, most notably the glyph of an eagle on his chest.

"An Eagle preacher," Aiden muttered as he caught up to Hobbes. "What's he going on about?"

The preacher raised his hands in the air. "And lo, our salvation from this prison will come from the forgiving eye of Jorus, not the condemning Eye of the Storm!"

"The Eagles are the biggest tribe out there," Hobbes replied to his friend. "They sell hope. Hope is about all we have these days."

"The Eye provides!" the preacher continued. "New wonders every day to aid us on the path! We are not to deviate from the path! We are-"

The preacher got interrupted as a motor backfired, smoke billowing out among the group. Laughter followed this, all emanating from a nearby table occupied by a group of young bikers.

Like all members of the Dog tribe, the bikers wore leather and spikes, tattoos and chains. They were all armed, some guns in plain view, some strapped to their cobbled-together bikes.

"Dogs don't play well with others," Hobbes remarked.

As if on cue, one dog tossed a half-empty bottle into the preacher's crowd. It missed hitting anyone, but it smashed on the ground in a mess, splashing booze on people's clothes. It just made the Dogs laugh more.

Aiden stepped forward. "Hey, looks like the Dogs are playing fetch!"

The Dogs ceased laughing. Their eyes homed in on Aiden and they immediately rose, some resting their hands on their strapped weapons.

"You think you're a funny man, little boy?" one of the Dogs, an especially large one, muttered as he crossed his arms over his thick chest. He sauntered up to the comparatively tiny Aiden. "Any other wise words you wanna get out?"

Aiden tapped his chin, pondering for a moment. Then a grin appeared. "Sure," Aiden reached into his pocket, pulling out a paint-faded and discolored Lego figure. He playfully tossed the toy over the Dog's shoulder. "Go get it, boy!"

That's all it took. The Dog, faster than one would expect, brought his large fist smashing into Aiden's face. Aiden, surprised, spun around and plummeted to the dusty ground. Hobbes, wide-eyed, brought his hands into a defensive stance as the surrounding crowd formed into a circle.

"Hey, back off!" Hobbes warned as two other dogs barreled down on him. One swung at Hobbes, but the young man swerved, avoiding the strike. He returned with a punch of his own, connecting with the Dog's jaw. The bigger man went down, but his buddies wasted no time in reacting. They charged and piled on Hobbes. All around them the crowd started cheering the fight on.

As the fight went on, an old man and his young protege emerged from the market, pausing at the scene before them. They were both clad in elegant robes, mostly in different shades of purple. They also showcased gold symbols woven into the fabric; more Eagles.

Jorus's wrinkled face warped as his lips formed into a sneer. He turned to his subordinate, Bastion, a rigid young man of Aiden and Hobbes's age with short-cropped hair. Burn scars covered most of Bastion's right side, arm and torso, peeking up past his neck above his collar.

"Shall we investigate?" Jorus asked. He strode forward, hands out. Bastion crossed his arms in contempt, but followed.

Meanwhile, the fight continued. Aiden got back to his feet and joined in the fight alongside his friend. Though the crowd seemed to cheer for the two young men, no-one lent a hand. They had Aiden and Hobbes outnumbered, and the Dogs were dangerously close to pulling their guns.

"Make way for Lord Jorus," Bastion ordered as they reached the fight. The crowd, turning and recognizing the elder Eagle, did as the young man said. Jorus and Bastion entered the circle of the fight.

"Friends. Neighbors," Jorus spoke aloud, quieting the crowd. "Why the violence on such a glorious day in the Eye?"

Though he had the crowd's attention, Jorus's voice did not halt the fight.

"Such physical acts of force are the way of the old world," Jorus continued. "Please, let us embrace another way."

The fight continued. The big Dog walloped Hobbes in the jaw who swung away and staggered towards Jorus, blood from his busted lips spitting outward onto Jorus's robe, dotting the Eagle insignia displayed on the Eagle leader's chest. Hobbes then slumped over.

One glance down at the blood told Jorus this tactic wasn't working. He leaned close to his young aide. "End this."

Four Dogs, the big leader included, descended upon the lone Aiden. He tried to fight them off, but failed miserably when seemingly out of nowhere a pair of hands, one scarred all over, yanked one of the Dogs off of him. Aiden then struggled to get himself clear, noticing the same scarred fist pass his eyeline and connect with another Dog's face, sending him flying backward. The same hand then gripped Aiden's shoulder and finally yanked him free of the two remaining Dogs, pulling him upward until Aiden found himself face-to-face with Jorus's sidekick.

Bastion noticed as Aiden tried not to focus on the young Eagle's scarring, but Bastion didn't particularly care. Instead, the young man whipped around and delivered a booted sidekick into the face of a charging Dog. That left only the big Dog leader remaining.

Aiden sighed. "Thanks. I was gonna-"

Still gripping Aiden's shoulder, Bastion whipped him around and released, sending Aiden flying into the approaching big Dog. The two connected and landed in a twisted pile. Bastion then planted his booted foot upon the Dog he'd just face-kicked and finally looked to Jorus. With all involved sprawled in the sand, the disturbance was at an end.

"You see where separation leads us?" Jorus strode forward, raising his hands higher. "Distrust runs rampant between the tribes! We need to work together. Do you see Eagles fighting like animals? No, we trust each other. And we want to trust you."

Aiden, Hobbes, and the Dogs struggled to their feet as Jorus continued. "The Eagles protect. The Eagles serve their own people."

Bastion returned to his master.

"Take young Bastion here," Jorus said, patting his protege's shoulder. "Life in the Eye has dealt him a harsh hand. He had nothing. But we gave him something to live for. He serves as a knight dedicated to the people, people like you."

The Dogs grumbled and retreated, dragging off their beaten comrades.

Hobbes rubbed his jaw, glaring at the silent Bastion. He spat some remaining blood into the sand at Bastion's feet. "Come on, Aiden. The stink of bullshit seems to waft around here."

Aiden and Hobbes turned from the Eagles, but froze when they saw Deacon stomping his way toward them.

"Jorus!" Deacon bellowed, approaching the Eagle leader.

Jorus sensed Bastion tense up just slightly, but he rested a reassuring hand on his protege's shoulder. "Ah, Deacon. Late to help your boy, but luckily I was-"

"Stop!" Deacon interrupted. "You're trying to brainwash the people I've sworn to protect!"

"Brainwash?" Jorus shrugged. "I merely-"

"And on my son, no less?"

"Young Aiden is free to choose-"

"Preach all the scams you want," Deacon snarled. "But you leave my people out of it. Understand?"

Aiden approached. "Dad, it's fine."

Deacon shot his son a petrifying stare. "Let's go."

They turned their backs on the Eagles, but then Deacon paused. He turned back to face Bastion, inches from his scarred face.

"And you," Deacon tried sizing up the younger Eagle. "Lay a hand on any of my tribesmen again and I'll kill you."

But Deacon's attempted intimidation did not faze Bastion. He merely stared straight back, motionless.

Jorus shook his head. "Threats of violence are unwarranted, dear Deacon. I invite your Pathfinders to find a new way, a better way." He extended a hand to see if Deacon would reciprocate. "We can achieve much as a unified tribe, my friend."

Deacon regarded Jorus's hand a moment, then swatted it away.

Bastion again tensed, and half drew a knife from his belt.

"You and your kind are no friends of mine," Deacon muttered.

Jorus once again placed a hand on Bastion's arm, halting him. "If that is your wish."

Bastion re-sheathed the knife.

"Come, Bastion," Jorus said. "We are clearly not wanted here. Let us find others who wish for our help."

Bastion continued a stare-off with Deacon a moment longer, then disconnected while showing the slightest little grin. Then the two Eagles left, some crowd people following.

Deacon led Aiden and Hobbes to the market's perimeter, and the trio walked in silence. But it wasn't long before Deacon grunted and halted, spinning around to face his son.

"Dammit, Aiden!" Deacon said. "I thought I taught you better than this! What were you thinking? I gave you a job to do while we were out on the run. You do it?"

"I-"

"No! Instead, I find you getting into trouble we can't afford!"

"I was trying to help!" Aiden countered.

"What if you'd gotten hurt?" Deacon asked. "We've got nothing of enough value right now to trade the Eagles in exchange for treating broken bones. Stop being selfish and think of the tribe for once."

"What's with you? What are you so mad about this?"

Deacon paused, but then stormed off.

"What happened on the run?" Aiden asked, catching up. "Did you not find anything?"

"We found plenty."

"So what happened?"

"The Dogs happened. The people you were just picking fights with killed four of our tribe today."

"But... but it's market day. The tribes are all here. The path should have been clear, right?"

"The Storm is never clear. They were out there. We had to fight for this one. That's that."

Deacon continued on as Aiden thought it over, distracted and not noticing Hobbes catch up.

"Well," Hobbes muttered. "That went well."

"Fight for this one..." Aiden repeated his father's words. "Seems we fight for everyone."

Aiden noticed then that they had stopped next to the kiosk with the dolls. There were more displayed. All their black-buttoned eyes, some goggled and some not, looked upward to the sky.

"Every little scrap. Every inch," Hobbes pondered.

"Huh?" Aiden became distracted, looking back at Larina's kiosk in the distance.

Hobbes sighed. "There must be a better way."

CHAPTER 3

By the time Aiden and Hobbes returned to camp, the sun had already set. Though the hour was getting late, Pathfinder tribe members of various ages were still out in number, and many waved their greeting at the pair's arrival.

The Pathfinders's charting and map work were second to none, and the other tribes often relied on their talents whenever the Eye was on the move.

The boys passed a group of men hard at work on vehicle repairs, cobbling together parts that they could. Most of the tools and tech they used was very rudimentary, scrounged from wherever possible, making do with anything they found.

Further down there were women cleaning clothing and fabrics, using water pumped from stills set in the back of more trucks. Near them, men and women toiled at food stations, taking fruits and vegetables from mobile gardens in the backs of other vehicles. They kept small animals- chickens, raccoons, lizards- nearby in small cages.

Beyond all that, Aiden and Hobbes neared another group composed of children sitting upon the dusty ground while the tribal elders recounted lessons and stories to them. It was that group where Aiden found Jonah.

"We survive this swirling cage that surrounds us," Jonah lectured the children, "but never, and I mean never, are you to enter the Storm Wall. Never."

A young girl eagerly raised her hand high in the air.

"Yes, dear?" Jonah nodded to her.

"I'm not afraid of the Storm," she declared.

"Oh, you're not, are you?" Jonah replied with a mock look of astonishment.

The girl shook her head with pride.

Jonah leaned forward slightly. "Well, it's not the Storm you need to be afraid of, girl. It's the things inside the Storm."

The girl suddenly didn't seem so sure of herself, but the other kids seemed completely enthralled with Jonah's storytelling.

"They're out there," Jonah continued. "Monsters."

The children scoffed, taking it in as entertainment. But Jonah paused for a somber look. It took a moment, but soon his grim face quieted them down.

"Scales. Fangs. Claws," Jonah continued. "Eyes that burn in the night. Some say the howls of the winds are actually the roars of beasts. And they are hungry."

Silence. The children stared wide-eyed.

"That's right!" Jonah pointed his finger. "They are hungry for all little boys and girls who venture into their Storm!"

He noticed a nearby girl was clutching one a doll from the market in her arms. He motioned for her to hand it to him, which she reluctantly did.

"And there are still other things in the Storm. Not monsters. Not men. Something in between. Stormwalkers."

Some children gasped as Jonah held the doll in front of him.

"Actual Stormwalkers, not these little trinkets, have not been unseen for a very long time." After tossing the doll back to its owner, he grinned. "But every so often, in the night's dark, they come and snatch away naughty children to feed to the real monsters out there!"

Jonah pointed his knobbly finger again at the Storm Wall for effect, and the children clapped. They then dispersed, which Aiden took as his cue to meet with his grandfather.

"Now, all of you behave!" called to the departing children. "Listen to your parents! Your elders know best. Dream free."

"See ya later, Aiden," Hobbes told his friend as he departed.

Jonah rose and hugged his grandson. "Aiden."

Aiden returned the hug, but then drew away when he saw a group of Pathfinders going over their recent acquisitions from the Dogs earlier.

"I saw your father," Jonah commented. "He stormed through here in quite a huff. What have you been up to?"

"I can tell you what I should have been doing!" Aiden countered. "If they had included me on the run, maybe we wouldn't have lost people to the Dogs today. I could have helped, but again I got left out. And again he gets angry with how I spend my time."

"He's your father, Aiden. He's trying to protect you. It's hard enough with the runs and warring with the tribes."

"Protect me? Why? I don't need protection."

"Because you are his son! I was the same with your mother, you know," Jonah sighed. "And that's why I know he's wrong. He needs to loosen his grip. But you need to learn to tighten yours and quit messing around with your friends."

Aiden thought about it. "Where is he?"

"In your tanker."

"Should I wear armor?"

"He's upset, not angry," Jonah winked. "Well, maybe just a helmet."

The vehicle that served as Deacon's and Aiden's home built out of a converted tanker truck, which included two separate tank cylinders attached to the truck cab, each cylinder cut into and used, the front one as a living space, the back as storage for supplies.

Without saying a word, Aiden bounded up the makeshift ladder and into the tanker-home. A cantankerous Deacon, arms crossed, standing immediately before him.

"Given up on knocking, have we?" Deacon asked.

"Next you'll be complaining I didn't wipe my feet," Aiden remarked.

Deacon remained grim. "You didn't."

Two large cushions sat in the middle of the room. Deacon motioned for his son to take a seat, and as the younger of the two did so, Deacon handed him a mug of water. Deacon sighed, pacing the room as Aiden drank his water. As he did, Deacon regarded the items adorning their home; junk found in the Storm, tools, and many, many charts pinned to walls and flattened on tables.

"About today," Deacon began.

"I know you mean well," Aiden cut in.

"I mean to groom you into what this tribe needs," Deacon said. "They depend on us, Aiden. And they can't depend on you if you're dead."

"Our family has taken care of the tribe since the beginning," Aiden reasoned. "I understand that. But these people know what they're doing."

"So you think they don't need leadership?" Deacon asked.

Aiden shrugged his shoulders.

Deacon burst out. "People need guidance! And there are wild Dogs out there!"

Aiden shook his head. "And we're just supposed to be the shepherds, huh?"

"It's how people are. They need a strong voice to sound despite the winds. They need leaders."

"You're starting to sound like the Eagles," Aiden muttered. "Next you'll be saying the Storm was our fault."

"Don't compare me to them, please. They're more lost than you are. Can't you just do as I ask?"

Aiden paused. "And what did mom want me to do?"

Deacon took a moment before speaking. "Things are getting worse every cycle. We're finding less and less to scavenge all the time. Something needs to change. And soon."

Deacon approached one chart pinned to the wall. He traced his finger along a penciled-in path that represented the trail of the Storm.

"You're not usually this out of it," Aiden noticed. "What's wrong?"

Deacon's finger stopped at a certain part of the map. He tapped the chart twice. "Look."

Aiden rose and approached, looking at what his father was showing. "I thought we had the new course of the Storm charted out weeks ago."

"We did," Deacon said. "But this is still troubling me."

The chart depicted a topographical map of the continent.

Many lines of pencil scrawled over the map, again and again, with only the occasional slight variation. Deacon's finger was tapping on the eastern coast of the land mass they lived upon.

"Later this cycle," Deacon said. "The Eye will travel beyond the coastline and out to sea."

"What?" Aiden gasped. "Why haven't you said anything to the others yet?"

"We're gonna feel the squeeze," Deacon replied. "Your grandfather and I have been debating over how to get us all ahead, close enough to the Storm Wall for a journey down the coast."

"And...?"

"And the Dogs are in the way," Deacon sighed. "After what happened today, we can't afford to confront them. Not anytime soon."

"So let them have the lead and raid everything before us? There'll be nothing left!"

"There'll be nothing left for *any* of the tribes. But most of the other tribes are better equipped to deal with those animals. I just don't like the tribes being forced so close. Too many birds in the cage."

"Like today," Aiden mumbled. "It's hard to act nice sometimes."

Staring at the chart, Aiden didn't notice the pang of guilt that rippled over Deacon for a moment.

"Yeah," Deacon agreed. "It is hard. But maybe we can't afford to be nice anymore."

CHAPTER 4

As the day came to a close, the market visitors returned to their camps. Vendors packed up their carts, vehicles and stalls. They would leave behind nothing.

Larina finished up with a rabbit carcass, using a large knife she held. Her two colleagues, Barb and Ivy, also young women from the Thorn tribe, folded up their belongings and unsold animals so they could return to camp.

"Larina, hurry," Ivy demanded. "I don't want to be the last to leave with those Dogs still out there."

"I know, I know," Larina replied as she moved on to folding up unsold clothing.

"And don't get any blood on those robes," Ivy continued. "It took all week to dye them and I don't want purple hands for the rest of the season from redoing them."

"Got it," Larina sighed. "Are these robes meant for the high priests?"

Barb shrugged. "So many Eagles calling themselves priests now I can't keep track anymore."

Larina smirked, but then noticed three Dogs approaching. Her smile quickly faded.

"As long as they keep wanting expensive robes and paying for them," Barb continued. "I don't really care. Men and their stupid fancy clothes."

"Oh no," Larina muttered.

The two other Thorn girls glanced to Larina, also spotting the approaching Dogs.

Two of the Dogs seemed to help the third along in between them, his arms over their shoulders. This shuffling Dog was Ted, and would have been an imposing man if he hadn't been drunk. He was overweight, but used that huskiness as an advantage to bully and belittle weaker tribes. Leader of the Dog tribe, Ted was not someone to get yourself in trouble with.

One of the other Dogs that helped him was Ted's brother, Vic. Built similar to his brother, Vic carried his more muscular weight with ease, and used in his work as a mechanic. Vic had a full, thick beard, which made him appear older than Ted, when he was in fact the younger of the two.

As the Dogs passed the Thorn girls, Ted suddenly broke free of his fellow Dogs and plodded over to the young women, Larina in particular.

"Hey, pretty lady," Ted said.

Larina continued to finish with her work, never breaking eye contact with Ted, who leaned on her worktable.

"You know," Ted continued. "I got a rip in my pants today. Was wonder'n if you could help me out?"

"Market's done," Larina said. "Have to wait til next gather."

"Oh, market's done, is it?" Ted scoffed. "Well, don't that work out well? Just so happens I laid claim to a whole crate 'a booze last raid. You're free 'ta join me."

"Not interested."

Ted's eyes narrowed. "I hear old Jorus is sending someone for a walk tonight. Should be quite a show, seeing the Storm swallow up one of those old fools."

He then regarded the other two Thorns present and grinned. "Three of you girls," he paused, drunkenly trying to count. "An' three of us! It's destiny! So what ya' say?"

"You're getting blood on your sleeve," Larina replied.

Ted looked down and raised his elbow from a pile of rabbit guts on the table. Vic and the other Dogs laughed. Ted turned red, but instead of exploding, barely saved face. He placed his hands on the table, fingers stretched in the rabbit remains.

"I'm used to getting blood on me, darlin'." He grinned.

With expert precision, Larina swiftly sank the knife she'd been holding into the wood grain of the table, directly between Ted's fingers.

"Even when it's your own blood?" she asked.

"Oh, you Thorns are a prickly bunch," Ted chuckled. "But I hear once you peel back the petals, all you bitches want is a nice big prick of your own-"

"Ok Teddy," Vic stepped forward, interrupting his brother as he tried to turn him away. "We get the point."

"Oh, she'll get my point," Ted argued. "And get your greasy hands offa' me!"

"Now, now boys," a voice sounded from behind them. Creed sauntered up from the rapidly dwindling crowd. He carried a duffel bag slung over his shoulder. "You wouldn't be causing these decent ladies any trouble now, would you?"

The Thorn girls quickly went back to their work, glad to have had the attention drawn from them.

"What if we were?" Ted growled. He pulled the fabric of

his vest aside to reveal a handgun tucked in his belt. "Pretty boy."

"Settle down, fellas," Creed said. "I just assumed after this morning's raid you'd be done causing trouble for one day."

All three Dogs laughed.

"We ain't never done causing trouble, Pathfinder," Vic replied. "This is our Eye you're living in, remember. Whoever makes the cars runs the show."

Creed nodded slowly as he lowered his bag to the ground. "Seems Deacon thinks otherwise," he said as he rummaged through it.

He then pulled a bloody pipe from the bag, the same bloody pipe Deacon used on the Dog earlier that day. He toyed with it in his hands.

"Thought you boys might want a souvenir from this morning," Creed said. "Since you Dogs didn't really bring anything home. Come to think of it, they didn't make it home themselves, either."

Creed dropped the pipe at Ted's feet. The Dogs almost snapped at this, until Vic stepped forward, placing a hand on his brother's chest to keep him at bay.

"It was a raid," he reasoned. "Theirs bested our guys for once."

"I suppose it's about time another tribe bested us on a raid," Ted relented with a snort. "Never thought it woulda' been you Pathfinder runts though."

Creed laughed, then turned and left. Once he'd gone, Ted picked up the pipe. He rolled it in his hands, feeling the weight of it.

Ted and Vic arrived at the Dog camp via a butchered Cadillac, a trail of black smoke spewing behind it.

The Dog camp was like a scrap yard. They had many scrapped vehicles parked around raging campfires where Dog tribe members were shouting, laughing and fighting with each other. Out of all the tribes, the Dogs collected the most tools and junk from the old world, and were more than capable of restoring most of them. But as skilled as they were, they were also savage and unruly.

The Cadillac lurched to a halt next to a rusted-out camper adorned with bones and skulls of various animals, even the odd human bone added for good measure. A cheer from the Dogs erupted, greeting Ted with admiration. It provided him with renewed balance and confidence, and Ted scrambled atop the camper with a bottle in one hand, the bloody pipe in the other.

"My Dogs!" Ted greeted. "I return to see less ugly faces than when I left! Are we not the top Dogs of the Eye?"

The crowd cheered again.

"Today, the most pathetic of the tribes took a stand against us," Ted continued. "And if *they* can, they all can!"

A couple Dogs in the crowd shook their fists, one of them shouting "Let's go teach 'em a lesson!"

Vic quickly took hold of the shouting Dog and head-butted him square in the face.

Ted laughed. "We could take out every tribe in the Eye without breaking a sweat!"

The Dogs roared their approval.

Ted shook his head. "We're the most generous, yet they label us as Dogs. So we spend and don't hoard. So we fight and don't cower. So we take and don't barter. So what? We grow strong! Snuffing out the tribes would be easy as snuffing out a fire!"

Ted then chucked his bottle into a nearby fire, the booze within igniting the flames into a momentary inferno, illuminating him in its orange glow.

"Next tribe that makes a salvage raid," Ted demanded, "we set an example! We'll be a show of force that'll ripple through the Eye. Remind the tribes that we will not be disrespected!"

Ted shook the bloody pipe high above, and the Dogs reveled in their approval.

Vic, however, took notice of the knot that formed in his gut. He stared at his brother as the image of fire filled his thoughts.

A fire that would threaten to consume them all.

CHAPTER 5

The Pathfinders had gathered together for the evening feast. Makeshift benches and tables jutted out from vehicles to serve as displays for the day's salvaged food. A fire burned brightly in the middle, illuminating the camp. Above the fire, a line of cans and other containers hung, their contents bubbling and boiling to the delight of hungry eyes. A guitar player strummed his old instrument, giving a sprinkle of tune over the tribe's chattering.

Jonah approached the tanker truck, carefully ascending the propped-up steps, waving away any who attempted to help him. Once up top, he firmly planted the end of his cane upon the metal deck four times, causing his fellow Pathfinders to surrender their attention to him. Aiden, Deacon and Isaiah sat at the end of a long table near the tanker.

"Yes, yes. Quiet now. Quiet," Jonah called. "Now I wish I could say this was a good day. Thanks to Deacon and his crew, we have a nice haul, as you can see. But the cost was great. We are missing four mouths tonight. We owe them and honor them for their sacrifice, and out of respect, their rations shall go to their families."

Several Pathfinders bowed their heads and sobbed lightly. Others were angry.

Deacon stood. "I know everyone is angry about how today went. But I do not want a repeat of last time. You hear me? The Dogs are a menace to all tribes in the Eye, not just us."

"Yes, thank you, Deacon," Jonah acknowledged.

"No one is to take any action, understood?" Deacon continued. "Not without my-"

"Thank you, Deacon," Jonah cut him off. "Everyone enjoy the feast. We ration again tomorrow to prepare for the next move. Eat up, rest well and dream free."

Deacon reluctantly sat. Everyone with a glass, a can, or whatever else passed as a drink container raised them high in the air together as one.

Larina sat on a barren, rocky hillside, her trusty spear laid flat next to her. All around her was a mix of rock, sand, and debris of the old world. The hillside overlooked an open field in the far distance that was slowly being swallowed by the Storm Wall. Larina watched as a far-off procession of Eagle priests carrying torches led an old man dressed in a white gown. It was hard for Larina to make out the detail at her distance, but the twinkle of the torches and contrast of the white gown were enough to tell her what was happening.

The Eagles were sending someone for a walk. A long-standing practice of the Eagles when tribe members got deemed unfit to contribute, usually due to sickness, they received the judgement of banishment. They had to venture into the Storm with no protection, fully aware that the sheer force of the weather would destroy them. When the time came, most Eagles went willingly, as if it was an honor.

"Enjoying the show?" the voice of Hobbes sounded behind her.

Startled, Larina grabbed for her spear, making Hobbes pause in his approach.

"Hey, come on now," Hobbes joked. "If I was gonna try something I would have stayed quiet, right?"

Larina stayed firm, making sure he saw her spear.

Hobbes, however, paid no more attention to it as he ambled past her defensive posture and sat next to her.

She hesitated, then sighed and placed the spear back down.

"No," Larina said.

"No, what?"

"No, I'm not enjoying the show?"

"Then why are you watching?"

Hobbes watched as, far ahead, the man in white stepped away from the priests. Though they were much too far away, Hobbes could tell the priests started a chant.

"I'm here to pay my respects," Larina said. "Airs was a good man. He always made me laugh at market. Why have you come to watch a man walk?"

"Airs was a Pathfinder once," Hobbes replied. "One of the few who took a turn at raising me. I was sad when he left to join the Eagles."

"I didn't know he was once a Pathfinder."

They could see the figure of Airs standing out before the

storm wall. The old man removed the gown, revealing a frail body eaten by radiation. He then kneeled naked in the sand and waited as the priests departed.

"After he breathed the clicking air, in a bunker a few years back," Hobbes said. "He got real sick. He saw more and more of the Eagle doctors until faith in the Storm was all he had."

Larina looked from the scene to Hobbes. "Your tribe is kind. I'm sorry you've lost so many."

"Sometimes I think the Dogs have the right idea," Hobbes continued. "You don't see them fearing death."

They watched silently then as the Storm crept ever closer to the old man.

"My name's H-"

"Hobbes, I know," she grinned "I've seen you before. I'm L-"

"Lana!"

"Larina."

"Larina! The scary girl at the market."

Larina laughed at that.

"So," Hobbes said. "You're a Thorn, huh? What's that like? Living with only women? No men around."

"You wouldn't understand."

"I'd like to."

She swatted him on the shoulder playfully.

"All right!" Hobbes laughed. "We're on the same side."

"So there are sides then."

"Well, as long as you don't want to barbecue me or brainwash me, then you're all right by me."

"You and the Bird tribe just like us because we don't raid your salvage sites."

33

"Why is that? You ladies never seem to hunt for old world scrap like we do."

"We live off what the land provides, here and now."

"So you *do* worship the Storm," Hobbes commented as he pointed at the Eagles who had left by Jeep. "Like them Eagles."

"No," Larina countered. "We believe in nature, in life, that's all. The Storm provides only death. The tribes cling to relics of the old world and depend on them. We are free from that burden."

"Without all those relics," Hobbes said, "the Eye would be a lot more empty, Larina. It's empty enough as it is."

The distant Airs then kneeled in the swirling dust as the wind and debris increased in strength. Finally, the Storm Wall reached the field and engulfed everything, swallowing Airs from sight.

Larina bowed her head. "The Storm will reveal its treasure soon."

"What do you mean?" Hobbes asked.

"I have a friend in the Bird tribe. Robin. She told me they found an old world tunnel along the eastern front of the Storm Wall," Larina explained. "The markings on it say there's a shelter inside. If you stay alert, it will show itself soon."

"Why are you telling me this?"

"I don't want the Eye to be empty," she said. "Besides, like you said, we are on the same side."

Unaware of his distant audience, Airs leaned forward and crawled within the dark chaotic winds of the Storm. The flying sand bit at his flesh and burned his frail skin. Soon he could move no further, and gasping at the dwindling amount of breathable air, he felt sand coat his throat and lungs. He reached outward, fell, and died, his body resting before a pair of booted feet. The figure which stood there remained motionless for some time in the savage winds until finally it turned and made its way back into the heart of the Storm.

CHAPTER 6

The feast the previous night had done a great job at raising the Pathfinders' spirits, despite the cost it had taken to get there. But the following day it was time to move on.

Aiden emerged from his tanker-home with a renewed sense of energy, but found himself confronted by Hobbes, who quickly shuffled him out of other Pathfinders's sights.

"And you're sure she wasn't just playing with you?" Aiden asked after Hobbes had filled him in on Larina's information.

"Aiden, I'm telling you," Hobbes pleaded, "she's honestly helping us out."

"I guess so. No way you could manage to sweet-talk a Thorn," Aiden smirked.

Aiden removed a folded-up map from his pocket and spread it out on the hood of a nearby truck cab. The map was a mess of odd landmarks and patterns scribbled onto it over the years.

"The Bird camp is east of the Storm Wall around here," Aiden pointed on the map. "So the shelter should sit by this ridge to the south."

Hobbes nodded. "Just imagine Deacon's face when we walk back in here with the haul of a lifetime!"

"But we can't do this alone," Aiden thought. "Just the two of us against-"

"Against whom?" Hobbes intercepted. "The Birds? Our tribes have been friends for generations. I'm sure we can work something out. You said it yourself: you're fed up with Deacon holding you back, right? Never including us on raids. This is our claim."

Aiden sighed. "I don't know if I hate it or like it when you're right."

Hobbes laughed.

"Okay," Aiden agreed. "If we find the road is still intact, we should make it by high sun if the Storm keeps up with us."

"And how do you plan to get there?" a third voice, Creed's voice, asked from above.

Aiden and Hobbes froze and looked up. Creed sat leisurely atop the roof of the truck cab. He kept his gaze on the sky above.

"We-," Aiden stammered. "Well, you see-"

"Yes, I do see," Creed finished for him. "I see you have a hole in your little plan. A prize raid to be sure, but no way to get there without asking dear Dad for a vehicle."

"Creed," Hobbes reasoned. "We weren't seriously considering doing this... I mean..."

"We were going to steal one," Aiden said.

"Borrow one," Hobbes corrected. "Or maybe-"

A set of keys suddenly dropped from Creed's open hand to Aiden's feet. "Clumsy me. I seem to have lost my keys."

"You're not gonna tell Deacon?" Aiden asked, picking up the keys.

"Listen, kid," Creed replied, "your father needs a wake-up call and I think this is the perfect way to give it to him. Just be careful with the truck, okay? It's been my home for a long time. And don't go looking in the glove box."

"Thanks," Aiden smiled. "Come on Hobbes, let's go."

"Yeah," Hobbes agreed. "Thank you, Creed."

The two headed off, not seeing the grin on Creed's face.

"Good luck," Creed chuckled.

A battered stretch of road snaked in and out of existence amidst the desolate wasteland. Creed's truck, also very battered, zoomed along the pitiful roadway, its large tires making easy work of debris littering the landscape.

Aiden sat at the wheel, Hobbes the passenger seat, inspecting a rifle. The two could barely hear each other over the roar of the decrepit engine.

"So what do you think we'll find?" Hobbes shouted.

"If it is a shelter, let's hope there's food," Aiden shouted back. "Are you sure this'll be a brand new find? Never scavenged?"

Hobbes double-checked the map spread on the dashboard. "It's new, all right; chart's clean for another mile or so in every direction. Who knows what's hidden here?"

Hobbes popped open the glove box.

"Creed's probably told Dad already," Aiden realized. "He's probably arranging a scouting party right now. He's gonna be mad when we get back."

"Forget the scouting party," Hobbes replied as he rooted around in the glove box. "He'll be arranging a celebration party for us when we return with months' worth of supplies."

"What are you doing?" Aiden noticed. "Creed said to stay out of there."

"If he really didn't want us to look," Hobbes reasoned, "he wouldn't have mentioned it."

Hobbes then removed an aged magazine from the glove box. It had a faded and brittle cover, but they could still make out the sight of a mostly naked woman on the cover. The title across the top read PLAYBOY. Both the guys regarded the magazine, and then shrugging, put it back.

CHAPTER 7

Built into the mound of a hilly landscape sat a military bunker, surrounded by the remnants of an old army base which the generations of the Storm's ever-violent conditions had mostly washed away.

Two people worked at the bunker's entrance, trying to break their way in. Both were members of the Bird tribe, as their names revealed. The smaller of the two, Robin, was a young woman, petite and red-headed. She wore an old hoodie and cargo pants that were weighed down by tools and gear.

Her companion was Crow, her brother. Crow was tall and slender with thick black hair. He wore a dingy jacket that was far too large for him.

"One, two, three," Robin ordered. "Pull!"

Crow threw his weight on the crowbar they were using to jimmy the hatch open. Finally, the metal latch gave way, and the hatch creaked open an inch at a time.

"I'm telling you this is a waste of time," Crow muttered as he caught his breath. "I bet they raided this place a long time ago."

"Well, we're here now," Robin reasoned. "Quit complaining and let's find out if you're right or not."

Robin moved to enter the hatch, but Crow grabbed her shoulder.

"Hold on!" he warned. "Remember to always check for clicking air."

Aside from the ever present danger of the Storm, rival tribes, and other hidden dangers of life in the Eye, there was also the threat of radiation to worry about. Many old factories, military bases and power plants still held remnant power from the Old World, a sickening power that claimed the lives of many tribes-people over the generations.

"Fine, hurry!" Robin groaned.

Crow pulled from his bag a battered and beaten device with a sensor on the front and display on top. When he activated it, the device gave off small clicks; a Geiger counter. Crow waved the counter around within the doorway of the hatch, but the clicking of the device remained the same, a slow steady pulse.

"See," Robin said. "It's good. Let's go!"

She practically dragged him into the dark entrance. The inside of the bunker was pitch black save for the single beam of light emanating from the hatchway, but even that vanished quickly as they wandered down the hall. Robin rummaged in her pockets, pulling out two small flashlights.

"This place smells bad," Robin remarked as she handed Crow a flashlight.

"What were you expecting?" Crow replied.

A sea of garbage littered the floor, and the pair had to fight back gagging as their feet disturbed the refuse, various putrid aromas being unleashed as they walked.

"We shouldn't stay long, Robin," Crow said. "This air is so foul."

"I've smelled worse," Robin scoffed. "Mainly you."

"Funny," Crow said as he rummaged through the clutter on various shelves and in cupboards they passed. Robin did the same, but after some time they were still coming up empty.

"Look at this junk," she complained. "It's all garbage!"

"We just started. Don't be so impatient."

Robin's flashlight beam passed over another open hatchway leading down a second hall. "Let's try down there."

She rushed down the hall, not waiting for Crow's reply.

"Wait!" Crow called after her. He hurried to catch up.

Robin hadn't gone far. She stood still just ahead.

"Don't do that," Crow ordered. "We need to be care-"

"Quiet!" Robin hissed. "Hear that?"

Crow listened and panicked internally when he heard a rustling sound from behind them. They whirled around but saw nothing other than some tipped-over plastic trays on a table. Crow turned back to Robin to suggest leaving, but found her to no longer be there.

"Robin?" he whispered. "Robin!"

Robin's hushed voice emanated from a doorway further down. "In here!"

Crow hurried through, furious. "What the hell you doing?"

"Finally found something," she replied as she pulled batteries from a pile of military-style crates. "Well, help me. Check the closet."

Crow shuffled over and inspected items in the closet shelving. There was a slim book which Crow carefully picked up, and it almost crumbled in his hands. "Hey, look at this."

"We can't eat a book, Crow."

Crow slowly opened the cover and read from the first entry;

Sergeant James Wolfe, October thirtieth, 2056. Thirteen months since the storm hit and our refuge is now more a prison than home. Simon says the storm should have died down mid-February, but that fucking thing keeps on turning.

Contact with shelters Bravo Sixteen and Delta Seventeen stopped today. If they are anything like us, it means they've heard the noises too. Out in the storm, voices, scratches at the hatch doors. Half of us have left, hoping to take their chances out there. Others had a final party in the munitions room. Heard the shots all night.

The generators are giving out as I write this. Soon it'll be lights out. Then I'll be a good soldier and retire.

Robin aimed her flashlight around the room, settling on a cot with a human-sized lump covered in blankets.

"Crow," she whispered. "Wanna check what's under there?"

He put down the book and approached the cot. He took a corner of blanket in hand and slowly pulled the covering away which revealed the decomposed corpse beneath. The body was dressed in a formal military uniform and awkwardly holding an ancient pistol in hand. A large hole in the skull told the story.

"They lost their minds stuck in here," Crow said. "Their shelter became their tomb."

"Just like the Eye," Robin said, not able to look away from the corpse. "Our shelter is also our tomb."

Crow tried to take the pistol, working it out of the corpse's hand. Finally it came free, and right then they heard a loud crash from elsewhere in the bunker that made Robin jump high in the air.

"What was that?" Robin squealed.

Crow gripped the pistol. "Come on, could be dinner."

They made their way further into the bunker, and eventually paused at a doorway labeled ARMORY, with sounds coming from within. Robin pulled a pocket knife and flicked it open. Crow nodded, and as they turned off their flashlights, the two stepped inside.

The armory contained racks holding the occasional rifle or ammo box. The number of usable materials was small, but possibly enough to outfit a few Birds. Robin and Crow collected what they could, but froze as two beams of light set upon them.

"Hands up!" a young man's voice rose out of the darkness. "Hands where we can see them!"

"Drop the knife, missy!" a second voice ordered.

"Don't come any closer!" Robin warned.

The light beams lowered then, and as Robin and Crow's eyes adjusted to the returned darkness, they saw Aiden and Hobbes ahead of them, weapons drawn. Aiden had a handgun while Hobbes supported a rifle cocked against his shoulder.

"This is our claim!" Robin said. "Get lost!"

"Relax, lady," Hobbes replied. "You're outgunned."

"Who are you people?" Crow asked.

"Pathfinders," Aiden said as he lowered his gun. "If we were Dogs or Eagles, wouldn't we have shot you by now?"

"Pathfinders?" Crow questioned. "How d'you know about-"

"Larina told us," Hobbes finished. "Said there might be a lot of loot here."

"Larina," Robin acknowledged. "Great."

This confused Crow. He looked to Robin. "You told a Thorn about this place?"

"Dove told me," Robin admitted. "I told Larina. She's a friend."

"We're all friends here," Aiden spoke. "I'm sure there's enough for both tribes if we look. But we better hurry before the Dogs find out."

Crow sighed as he lowered his newly gained pistol.

"What are you doing?" Robin demanded.

"We'd never hear the end of it if we killed a couple Pathfinders," Crow replied. "There's no point fighting until we find something worth fighting over."

Robin reluctantly put her knife away. "Fine."

"We've been through the stores down this side," Hobbes said. "Barely even a can of beans. Generator's dead and fuel cans are empty."

"Best we could find was some ammo," Aiden added. "You two have any luck?"

Robin shivered, thinking back to the corpse in the other room. "Nothing much, no."

"Let's keep looking then," Aiden reasoned. "This place smells bad, but there are a lot of rooms to sort-"

A loud whine echoed from the bunker entrance, the hatch being swung open and then closed. The four looked to one another, alarmed.

"Anyone else knows you're here?" Aiden asked the Birds.

"No," Crow said. "Just us."

Voices became audible, gruff and loud. The sound of thrown junk and debris got louder and closer.

"We're too late," Aiden whispered. "Dogs."

Crow shook his head. "Their convoy is too far west right now. Even if they found out, no way they'd get here so soon."

"Unless they were tipped off," Aiden answered.

The clanging increased. The four drew their weapons once again.

Ted, Vic and several accompanying Dogs made their way down the bunker corridor.

"Come out wherever you are!" Ted called as he banged the bloody pipe against the metal fixtures on the walls. "We heard some poor Pathfinders were in here all alone. We know you're here! Let's set the score right!"

It was dark, and the Dogs didn't carry flashlights. They had to peer carefully in the blackness.

A shadow of movement caught Ted's attention. "There! Back there!"

He raised his handgun and fired a shot, which clanged off the wall just shy of Robin's face. She dove behind a crate for better cover, followed by Hobbes and Crow. The other Dogs then followed up with shots of their own.

"Go! Go! Go!" Aiden ordered as he passed the others and advanced up the corridor, sticking behind crates and open hatch doors.

The Dogs also made their advance up the corridor, firing blindly as they went, laughing the whole way.

"This happens when you mess with the big dogs, boys," Ted told his Dogs. "We'll send their heads back to Deacon when we're done here!"

Aiden leaned out from behind a door and fired. One of the Dogs took the bullet to his neck and collapsed with a startled scream. The Dogs returned fire, and as Aiden and Hobbes kept firing back, Robin and Crow got caught in the middle. They crept along, searching for another way out. Dodging a second hail of Dog gunfire, Crow came upon a ladder set in the wall marked SURFACE ACCESS B. He tried to push the ladder's hatch open but it wouldn't budge.

"Help me with this!" he cried.

The Dogs continued their blind shots at their unseen enemy, but then Ted stopped and pulled a grenade from his belt. He smiled with menace as he moved to pull the pin. But then Vic reached over and snatched the grenade from his brother.

"The hell you think you're doin'?" Vic demanded.

"Piss off, Vic," Ted replied. "Better end them before they finish our boys."

"Don't be stupid. A grenade in here would take us all out."

"You know, I'm getting real tired of your shit, Vic," Ted replied. "You wanna be Alpha? Huh, big guy?"

"Forget it," Vic groaned. "I'll end this myself."

Fearless, Vic left his fellow Dogs and headed up the corridor.

The ladder hatch finally groaned in protest as both Crow and Robin got it pushed open. Outside lights beamed down upon them, and Robin climbed up while Crow hopped back down. He ran to Aiden and Hobbes.

"It's open!" Crow said. "Let's go!"

The three of them rushed back to the ladder. Reaching it first, Hobbes slung his rifle over his shoulder and climbed to the outside. Aiden began climbing next when he and Crow spotted Vic approaching.

"Go!" Crow ordered as he drew his pistol.

Aiden climbed.

Vic then steamed up the corridor, his eyes set on Crow.

Crow took aim and pulled his trigger, but instead of firing, the clicking hammer caused the old, decrepit gun to mostly fall apart in his hand. Then the much larger Vic pounced on him. Vic grabbed Crow by the skull with one hand and smashed the Bird's face upon the ladder rungs.

Outside and above, Aiden got to his feet with the aid of Hobbes and Robin.

"Crow?" Robin asked, but the look on Aiden's face told her. Just like that, he was gone.

"I'm sorry, Robin," Aiden muttered.

Robin almost snapped then, but the three of them heard the grunting of Vic making his way up the ladder. Without a word, Robin threw herself upon the hatch door. Then Aiden and Hobbes joined her, and their combined weight finally forced the door closed again just as they saw the face of Vic reaching them.

He gave out a loud growl as the hatch locked shut under them.

A loud creak then sounded from an overhang above the three, and as they looked up, they had to dive backward to avoid the falling debris. Amidst the wreckage was a fin-shaped object with a decal printed on the side; THE NEMO.

Aiden stared at the strange object for a moment, then looked up to inspect the remaining wreckage atop the overhang above.

There was the smoking wreck of a small aircraft, crashed upon the hillside bunker's rear surface. It hadn't been visible from the bunker's front entrance, but from where they now stood it was in plain view. Aiden, Hobbes, and Robin stared in awe.

"What're you waiting for, idiots?" Ted's voice sounded from below the ladder hatch. "Go around!"

"The front hatch!" Hobbes cried.

Robin was then off in a flash, her small, determined form vanishing over the dune.

On an adjacent ridge overlooking the bunker rested another Dog. He laid flat in the sand, eyes staring down the scope of his rifle, keeping watch on the scene. He spotted Robin darting across the sand and took care to line his crosshairs upon her. His finger almost touched the trigger, but someone suddenly yanked the Dog to his feet. He gave a painful yelp as his attacker delivered a punch to his face, then whimpered as a powerful hand wrapped in bandaging closed on his throat. There was a crunch, and he went limp. The attacker then took the Dog's rifle in hand.

The front of the bunker had two Dog trucks parked outside, along with Creed's truck where Aiden and Hobbes had left it. Another lone Dog sat in one truck, reading the magazine he'd pilfered from Creed's glove box. A shot rang out, and the Dog lurched sideways as the bullet found its mark. He fell limply for the vehicle.

Soon after, Robin rounded the hill bend. She entered the second Dog truck, started the engine, and drove full speed at the bunker's entrance.

The truck collided with the entrance hatch just as a Dog tried to exit, and crushed him. The hatch then became a mangled wreck of truck and hatch door, blocked up for good without some manpower to move it from the outside. Ted, Vic and the other Dogs were now trapped inside.

Robin was safe. She panted heavily, then broke down and sobbed against the steering wheel.

Hobbes headed for the entrance, but stopped when he noticed Aiden wasn't following. He found his friend staring up at the wrecked plane.

"It looks like it crashed," Aiden said. "Recently."

"That's impossible," Hobbes scoffed. "There's no such thing as working flying machines outside of books."

"But here it is."

Aiden climbed the hill toward the plane. The thick smoke still rising from it didn't make the approach easy. But soon he made it up to the crumpled nose of the plane. He clambered onto it and peeked into the cracked cockpit window.

His eyes widened in shock.

"What is it?" Hobbes called from below. "Something in there?"

Aiden was looking at a young, dark-haired woman slouched unconscious, or worse, in the pilot seat.

"It's a girl," Aiden continued to stare. "There's a girl in here!"

CHAPTER 8

20 YEARS PRIOR

Deacon hiked toward the Pathfinder camp dressed in the usual many layers of protective clothing and carried a large pack on his back. As he pulled down his face scarf, revealing a younger but still grizzled face, he regarded the camp ahead with a smile.

As Deacon walked through the camp, he greeted its tribe members when they passed. Soon, he came upon Aiden and Hobbes, toddlers playing and climbing on the shell of an old truck.

"Poppa!" little Aiden called as he noticed his father. "Poppa's back!"

The two boys raced to him, and Deacon swept Aiden up in his free arm. "There's my boy! I've missed you."

"Have you brought more stories?" Aiden asked. "Can we hear about your adventure?"

Deacon pulled a can of beans out of his bag and tossed it to Hobbes. The little guy caught it and ran off excitedly.

"There's lots of time for stories, Aiden," Deacon replied, "if you've been a good boy for your mother."

"I've been good!" Aiden exclaimed. "Grandpa's been letting me work in the gardens with him and says I'll be big enough to take to market with him soon."

"Big enough?" Deacon scoffed, feigning pain as he shifted Aiden's weight upon his arm. "Well, you've definitely gotten bigger while I've been away. Your mother feeding you well?"

Aiden quieted a little. "Mom's not feeling good, so Grandpa feeds me."

"Not feeling well, huh?" Deacon wondered. "Maybe she'll feel better when she sees me."

Aiden nodded his head enthusiastically and together they approached the tanker truck. Deacon then noticed Jonah waiting outside, conversing with the doctor, Reeves, a tall, thin man on the brink of his middle years. He wore a pair of bent glasses that barely stayed on his nose.

Deacon's smile faded as he approached, and he set little Aiden back on the ground. Kneeling, he then pulled a small Stormwalker doll out of his pocket. The doll had the familiar tattered cloth clothing and broken glass goggles.

"Here," Deacon told his son, handing him the doll. "Thought you might like this."

"A Stormwalker!" Aiden lit up. "But mom said I shouldn't have one."

"Why's that?"

"She says they're dangerous."

"Only the real ones," Deacon managed a smile. "Now go show your friends, okay? I'm gonna say hi to your mother."

Aiden raced off, Stormwalker doll held high above him. Deacon watched him leave, then turned to the others.

Jonah greeted his son-in-law by placing his hands on both Deacon's shoulders. "Welcome back, Deacon."

"Jonah," Deacon replied simply.

"I wondered if you'd return this time."

"I was going to," Deacon said, adjusting the bag on his shoulder. "And with enough supplies to help the tribe for another season."

Jonah sighed. "Supplies are helpful, but you do more good here than you do out there. You can't keep going off like this. Your family-"

"I just arrived," Deacon interjected. "I'm tired. I'm dirty. I just want to see Jade, all right?"

Deacon stepped toward his tanker, but the doctor stepped in the way, halting him.

"Deacon, wait," Reeves muttered.

Deacon knew something was wrong. "What is it?"

"I'm sorry to say this," Reeves replied. "Your wife has fallen ill."

"I know. Aiden told me. I've got cold medication I found out there-"

"Aiden doesn't understand. It's not just a cold."

"What exactly are you saying?"

"The kids were hungry," Jonah sighed. "The tribe was hungry. You weren't here. So, a week ago, she went on a raid."

"Where?"

"Just food gathering with a few other Pathfinders. The Eye had revealed a new ruin," Jonah shook his head. "It was the clicking air. She breathed the clicking air."

Deacon stared. "How much? How long was she exposed?"

"Long enough," the doctor replied.

Deacon pushed past them and entered the tanker.

53

They'd covered the windows, blocking most of the light within. Only the faintest orange glow filtered in. Jade, Deacon's loving wife, was curled upon the bed within the gloom, long brown hair limp around her. Her green eyes had sunken, her face withered and thin from radiation sickness. Deacon knelt to the floor next to the bed frame.

"Jade," he spoke softly. "Jade, it's me."

Jade's eyes opened slowly, and she managed a smile. "Deacon."

"I'm home. It took longer than I thought, but I'm home."

"It's okay."

She reached with a delicate hand and stroked Deacon's cheek. Adorned on her thin finger, barely remaining in place, was the jade ring. He held his hand over hers.

"You're gonna be all right," Deacon said.

"Sure I will," she replied. "But until then, will you stay?"

"Yes. Of course."

"Promise me you'll keep your promise," Jade whispered. "And take care of our son."

Deacon resisted the tears forming in his eyes and nodded.

"You are the one," Jade continued. "The only one strong enough to see us through-"

A fit of deep coughing overwhelmed her, and Deacon stroked her shoulder.

"It's okay, I promise," he whispered. "Just rest, please. I'm not going anywhere."

Once her coughing subsided, Deacon kissed his wife.

Jade forced a weak smile. "I don't think I can say the same. Here."

She pulled the ring from her finger with ease, her withered

hand gladly giving it up. The ring almost looked gargantuan in her hand.

Deacon grimaced. "You're giving up."

"I'm *grateful*," she smiled. "You've given me a happy life, my husband. We had our doubts, in the beginning. It was a big change, Father and I coming here. But we made it work. And I love you for it. Keep this until we are together again."

"I will," Deacon agreed through tears. "Then it will go to Aiden."

"Take care of him."

"Always."

"He's meant to lead, Deacon. He'll lead our people one day, lead them into a better future."

"I'll make sure he's ready. It won't be easy."

"It never is. But it must be done. It's the only way."

Deacon nodded. "For a better future."

"A future I won't see," Jade said as she coughed again. "But I *will* be with you. Always."

Jonah and the doctor waited outside as Deacon emerged from the tanker, his feet heavy.

"How long you think she has?" Deacon asked without looking at them.

"Days, maybe," Reeves replied. "And they will not be good days."

"And there's nothing...?"

The doctor shook his head.

"They were all exposed," Jonah said. "The whole party. The others have all died. I think she's been holding on. For you."

"I have new clickers in my bag," Deacon shook his head. "If they'd just waited-"

"We take that chance every time we leave the camp," the elder Pathfinder said. "Except maybe you. You always seem to come out unscathed."

"I learned from her," Deacon muttered. "Like she learned from you. I've just been lucky."

"Perhaps."

"She's your daughter," Deacon glared. "Why did you let her go?"

Instead of going on the defense, the old man softened. "You think I wouldn't give anything in the Eye to be laying there instead of her? I want to blame you, Deacon. I really do. But she was bold long before she met you. And Storm help me if my grandson doesn't end up the same."

"Aiden," Deacon pondered.

"If you leave again, he'll be lost."

Deacon sighed, looking up to the calm sky. He noted where the calm of the Eye ended, where the violent dancing winds of the Storm Wall began.

"Look around," Jonah instructed. "What do you see?"

Deacon observed the Pathfinders milling about the camp at their different tasks.

"What do you see?" Jonah repeated.

"Pathfinders," Deacon answered.

"People, Deacon," Jonah countered. "Sad, hungry, lost people. Without a path to follow, how can we call ourselves Pathfinders?"

"You want me to provide that path."

"To them, you are the strongest here. You provide. You protect. Even the Dogs know to keep their distance from you, mostly."

"It's true," Reeves added. "Some Eagles have even spoken

of joining the Pathfinders if you were to take charge. You have a way of making waves in the Eye."

Jonah nodded. "This tribe needs your leadership. I know it. You know it. Jade knows it."

Aiden ran up to them then. "Can I say goodnight to Mom?"

Reeves nodded. "But don't disturb her for too long."

"Okay!" Aiden said as he entered the tanker.

Deacon watched the entrance of the tanker for some time. And then, finally, "I had to keep my first promise, Jonah. My promise to her. I had to keep the lines open, as we agreed. But you're right. Time to put that promise behind me. I'm not going out there anymore. The Eye is my home."

Deacon, Jonah, and Reeves were in the tanker. Jonah had his shirt off, the doctor inspecting him, much to Jonah's dismay.

"I told you, I'm fine," Jonah grumbled through his beard.

"You say that every time you meet with Doc Reeves," Deacon commented.

"Well," Jonah said, "that's cuz it don't ever change."

"I wish everyone was healthy as you, Jonah," Reeves said. "Cough for me."

Jonah did, but the coughing got deeper and uncontrolled. He didn't notice the look the doctor shared with Deacon.

"Okay," Reeves continued. "You can put your shirt back on. So how is Aiden doing? I heard he got into a bit of a scrap at the market."

"I almost wish he *had* broken something," Deacon replied. "Just to teach him there are bigger things than his ego."

Jonah finished buttoning his shirt. "He's like his mother."

"Or his father," the doctor smirked as he packed his bag and headed for the door. He then paused, patting Jonah's shoulder. "I'll check on you in a few days. Stay rested and try to avoid any sudden shocks, okay?"

Suddenly the door burst open, and everyone jumped back. Hobbes bounded into the room, frantic. He was completely out of breath.

"Hobbes?" Deacon asked. "Where have you two-"

"Hurry!" Hobbes shouted. "You gotta see this!"

Then he took off again. The others glanced at each other, then followed.

As they exited the tanker, they found Aiden approaching them. The tribe had crowded around him, gawking at what he carried in his arms.

The girl.

Petite, dark-haired, similar in age to Aiden, she wore a well-kept uniform of a solid orange color. It was unlike anything anyone in the Eye normally wore. She was still unconscious. Aiden struggled as he approached his father and grandfather. They both glared at him. All Aiden could do was deliver a sheepish smile.

CHAPTER 9

They placed the girl in Aiden's bed in the tanker. Aiden, Hobbes, Deacon, Jonah and Reeves stood around the bed, watching and pondering the new circumstances.

"She must have locked herself in there to escape the Dogs," Reeves reasoned. "If she couldn't get into the bunker there'd be nowhere else to hide."

"But that plane hadn't been sitting out in the Storm for years," Hobbes replied. "There was no rust. No water damage. No stripped paint. It was still smoking."

Jonah nodded. "Planes don't like to sit still. They like to fly."

"You think she flew that thing?" Aiden asked.

"It makes sense!" Hobbes said. "It looked like a crash. A recent one."

"And just her?" Aiden continued. "Alone? Flying that thing?"

"We'll ask her," Deacon said.

"Not right now," Reeves interjected. "She's out. Head trauma from this supposed crash, I'd wager."

"We're not asking the big question here," Deacon stated. "If she flew that plane, where did she fly it from?"

Jonah smiled. "He's right."

"The Eagles?" Hobbes wondered. "I'm sure they have nothing like a plane."

"No one does," Reeves said.

Jonah nodded. "No one we've met."

"Another tribe?" Reeves asked. "Where? The Eye is only so big."

Jonah looked to Aiden. "Exactly."

Aiden's eyes widened as he realized what Jonah was hinting at. "If there is another tribe out there, they're not in the Eye. She came from beyond the Storm."

Deacon became alarmed. He glared at Jonah. "You've thought about this. You claim this girl-"

"Flew here from outside the Storm, yes," Jonah agreed. "That means there is some land out there, somewhere. Somewhere safe."

"That's a serious statement, Jonah," Deacon said. "I need to say something to the tribe. They're waiting."

Reeves spoke, "We won't know anything until she wakes. I should take her to the Eagles for proper treat-"

"No," Jonah cut him off. "I think it best she stays here. Last thing we need is Jorus getting his claws on her."

"It's your call, Jonah," the doctor shrugged. "Dream free."

"Dream free, doc."

Reeves left. Deacon, Hobbes, and Jonah headed for the exit, but Aiden stayed back.

"I want to stay with her," Aiden said. "In case she wakes, I mean."

"Of course," Jonah smiled. Then they left.

Aiden sat next to the bed, pondering. The girl had not moved or made a sound. Yet to Aiden, he had never seen someone who seemed so alive.

As the others emerged into the night air, the entire Pathfinder tribe confronted them.

"What's happened?" many of them asked as if in unison.

"There's nothing to worry about," Deacon said. "A girl, not of this tribe, is under our care for now."

"Which tribe is she from?" someone asked.

"Are the Dogs part of it?" asked another.

Deacon shook his head. "Go back to your business."

He continued forward, ignoring all further questions. Jonah tried to keep pace.

"You must tell them more sometime," the elder Pathfinder whispered.

"But not right now," Deacon muttered back.

"What's your plan then?"

Deacon shook his head. "I really don't know."

CHAPTER 10

The Storm surrounded Aiden. Violent, dark and menacing, the Storm swirled all around him, threatening to claim his life in its ever-shifting maw. Aiden struggled to make his way through it. He staggered, pushed forward, and staggered more. He soon fell to his knees, unable to see through the wall of wind and dust. He tried to cover his eyes, but it was too much. Why hadn't he brought goggles?

He crawled along the ground, hands tracing as he searched for anything he could take hold of in the increasingly inky blackness. Then his hand froze as it came into contact with something; a boot.

Someone was wearing the boot. Above the boot was a mass of rags that began and ended beyond Aiden's vision. He forced himself up as he tried to make out the figure before him. Finally, he discerned the tall, imposing form of what he had heard legends of his whole life; a Storm Walker.

Clad in robes and rags from head to toe, even the figure's face was hidden from view, eyes concealed by a pair of tinted goggles. The Storm Walker stood like a statue before Aiden, its identity completely hidden beneath the goggles and face bandages.

Aiden backed away, only to realize they were not alone. More Stormwalkers surrounded them, silent and stoic, a small army of faceless, voiceless forms. They had Aiden boxed in. Thay had him trapped.

Aiden woke with a start as a slender hand touched his own. His eyes fluttered open to find the very awake face of the girl. She blinked at him.

"Uh, hi," Aiden gulped. "You're awake."

The girl said nothing.

Uncomfortable with her silence, Aiden tried to stand.

"Bhí tú i do chodladh," the girl spoke.

Aiden stopped and looked at her, puzzled. "What?"

"Fuair tú dom," the girl continued. "Go raibh maith agat."

"No way," Aiden whispered. "I'm Aiden. You were in a, well, a plane. I was hoping you'd tell me where you're from."

The girl stared blankly at him for a moment, and then "Níl sé tábhachtach."

Aiden scratched his head. "Great. Dad won't like this."

Later, everyone gathered around the room; Aiden, Deacon, Jonah, Hobbes, Isaiah, and Creed, all awaiting to hear the girl's grand speech. But it never came.

"Like I said," Aiden reasoned, "she's not gonna be able to answer questions. She can't speak our language."

"How's that even possible?" Isaiah asked. "Ours is the only language left, apart from in books."

"It tells us she is definitely not from the Eye," Jonah stated.

"Tá tú ar an mbóthar ceart," the girl said, slightly smiling.

"Well, she came from somewhere!" Deacon said, ignoring her. "We'll check with the other tribes. Ask them if they're

63

missing a girl in weird orange clothes. And check with the Eagles, but be discreet. We don't want Jorus learning of this."

"Listen to me," Jonah addressed everyone, though his eyes were on Deacon. "We must follow this. She came from beyond the Storm, I'm sure of it."

"I'm sorry, Jonah," Deacon replied. "We just can't afford to follow legends."

"We could go back to the plane," Jonah said. "Backtrack from there."

"Is mian liom a raibh mé in ann a bheith cabhrú le níos mó," she replied.

Deacon raised his arms in defeat. "What if that plane spun around as it crashed, huh? Who knows which direction is correct? This is foolish!"

"But what if it's not?" Jonah asked.

Creed had been silent until then, but nodded at Jonah's point. "She got through the Storm. Maybe, if she could…?"

Isaiah shook his head. "Everyone who goes beyond the Storm has died. The Eagles' Walks prove that!"

"We don't know," Hobbes said. "Not for sure."

"Quiet!" Deacon ordered. "I agree this is confusing, but let's not give into wild hopes just yet. Aiden, get her something to eat. The rest of you will know more when we figure this out."

Everyone but Aiden and the girl left, most in disappointment. Once they were alone, Aiden guided her to a chair to sit. He then went about preparing her something to eat.

"You're probably hungry," he said over his shoulder. "Hope you're ok with canned food."

"Níl i ndáiríre ach beidh sé a dhéanamh," she replied.

"You know, you've caused a lot of commotion out here, girlie."

"Cailín-ie?" she asked.

Aiden then returned to her with two bowls filled with canned gruel. He handed her one bowl and sat across from her.

"I don't even know what to call you," he said as he watched her eat. "You must have a name. Wish you could tell me what it is."

"Ba mhaith liom a d'fhéadfaí tú a figiúr ach é amach," she said through a mouthful of food.

Aiden watched her, pondering. Then, finally, getting a genius idea, he slapped his own knee in excitement.

"I got it!" he exclaimed. "Nemo!"

She just looked at him confused.

"Your plane! It was called the Nemo, I saw," he explained. "That's it, then. I'll call you Nemo."

Nemo shrugged. "Cibé rud a."

Aiden pointed at her. "Nemo," he said, then pointed at himself. "Aiden. Get it?"

Nemo smiled. "Aiden."

Aiden smiled right back.

CHAPTER 11

As leader of the Eagle tribe, Jorus had a self-appointed privilege to his own extravagant tent, a yurt that Eagles had to set up and take down every time the tribe moved. And within the yurt, amidst his fancy and colorful fabrics, trinkets, art pieces and books, Jorus also had his own throne, which he sat upon with pride. He read from one of his newly gained books, a tattered hardcover of a 2032 Student Yearbook, when Bastion abruptly entered.

"My lord," Bastion spoke as he approached the throne. "I have news."

Jorus clapped the book shut. "You know I don't like my reading being interrupted."

Bastion hesitantly nodded. "I've received word from the Pathfinder tribe. They recovered a young woman from-"

"I know of the interloper," Jorus interrupted. "You forget I have eyes of my own throughout the tribes."

"They seek our wisdom," Bastion continued. "The girl speaks a language unknown to all. But no one in the Eye speaks a different language, not since the Storm cleansed the old world. Deacon knows this. Should we provide our library of knowledge?"

"We will do no such thing!" Jorus demanded. "We will not encourage this matter. If no one knows her language, it is because it is a dead language. It is blasphemy to speak them aloud in the Storm. Deacon can peddle his problems elsewhere."

Bastion stepped forward, then paused. But then, thinking better of it, he continued. "My lord, what if we can do some real good here? What if we are meant to aid them?"

Jorus stood and let his robes flow and dangle around him as if rolling out his own personal carpet. He wandered to his bookshelves and eyed all the books he's collected over the years. He then placed the one he'd been reading back in its place.

"Long ago, there were no tribes," Jorus said as he looked over his treasures. "We wandered without cause, without direction. Savage. Lost in the winds. If it weren't for my predecessors, we would have no Eagle tribe. The Eagles united us, made us strong. We were the rock that anchored humanity in the Storm. We gave people hope because we never wavered. I am not about to waver now."

The elder Eagle approached his protege and placed his hand on the young man's shoulder. "Do not worry. Deacon tests me with riddles, but I have eyes and ears within the tribes. If anything stirs I shall know of it."

Jorus headed for his tent's exit. "Perhaps this is a sign. I feel change is long overdue regarding Deacon's lead of the Pathfinders."

Bastion blindly followed.

In the still of night, Deacon emerged from his tanker dressed for desert travel. He looked around and noted the sparse camp at the late hour. But, just in case, he pulled his scarf up over his face.

A dirt bike was parked nearby. It had a small trailer latched to it, with a bundle of what appeared to be supplies, wrapped in a tarp for desert travel. As he sat upon the bike, he glanced back and spotted Jonah, standing in the shadows and leaning on his cane. Deacon nodded to the old man, but Jonah did not return the gesture. Instead, he marched up to Deacon, the wrinkles in his face strained with tension.

"We've talked about this," Jonah scowled. "The tribe comes first. And yet here you are, heading out once again. You gave your word, remember?"

Deacon reached into his tunic and pulled out the jade ring. He held it directly before Jonah's eyes.

"I gave her my word too," Deacon said. "This is a promise I need to keep, for Aiden. The girl changes things. I have to go, one more time. Then I'm done."

Jonah nodded, unconvinced. "Then you're all set here. Be careful."

Then he watched as Deacon placed the ring back in its spot, revved his bike, pulled on a pair of goggles, and drove out of the camp.

Jonah then stepped back into the shadows, blending with the night.

CHAPTER 12

Robin stood alone on the outskirts of her camp. The night sky illuminated the stars above. The twinkling lights held her focus for what seemed like hours.

She had stood in that spot since returning to the Bird camp earlier that day.

The squawking and crying of birds were a constant sound behind her. The Bird tribe, aptly named for their use of birds in their daily lives, kept their namesake in a huge aviary in the middle of the camp. Whenever a Bird tribesman left camp, it was customary to bring their life bird with them. Some had great birds of prey like hawks and falcons, while many others shared their lives with smaller breeds like sparrows and chickadees. Robin had her namesake, a small robin that often accompanied her to market.

Her brother had had his own crow, and she decided she was glad they'd not brought their birds with them to the bunker. The crow had not endured the death of its master, and she was happy for that at least.

Although the constant drone of bird noise did not pry her

from her thoughts, it was the approach of people that drew Robin's attention. She turned and found her two friends, Sparrow and Finch, approaching.

Sparrow was the same age as Robin. They were lifelong friends who had always had their camp spaces next to each other. While Robin's hair was a long and vivid red, Sparrow sported golden blonde locks tied into a ponytail.

Finch was near middle-aged, thin and mousy looking. They often overlooked him as a weakling, but Robin always knew that what he lacked in strength he made up for in brains. He was the Bird tribe's resident biologist, and he kept records of their bird kin and other life forms occasionally seen in the Eye. Finch also acted as a surrogate father to both Robin and Sparrow the past few years, ever since their parents died on salvage raids. Though he had let them go on their own as she, Crow and Sparrow aged, Robin knew that considering Crow's death, he would be there in an instant.

"Robin," Sparrow muttered as they reached her. She took Robin in her arms, and the two hugged.

"I'm so sorry," Finch said. "Are you all right out here?"

Robin nodded as she also hugged Finch. "Yeah. Just taking it all in, you know?"

"The ceremony was nice," Sparrow said. "Even without him actually there for it."

Robin shook her head. "The Eye has long passed beyond that bunker. The Storm would have been too much, not to mention Dogs in the area. No, this way was safer. Crow would have done the same."

"I guess it's time then," Finch said.

Robin sighed. It was the part she'd been trying to put off. But it had to be done, both for her sake and his bird's. She nodded, and the three of them returned to the camp. As they reached the camp's center, the rest of the Birds gathered as they saw what was about to happen.

It was a communal act of the Bird tribe, a group effort to give back to the Storm that ruled over them.

Robin reached the aviary. She scanned over the dozens of birds within, watching many of them fly back and forth while many more just stared right back at her. She spotted her own Robin and smiled as it hopped along a branch, playing with Sparrow's namesake and other small birds. Soon, though, she found the crow. It stood still as stone, already gazing at her. The common belief in the Bird tribe was that their bird kin were well aware, when it was time to be returned, that their masters were gone or unable to life-share with them anymore. This seemed no different. The crow knew.

"Crow," Robin spoke as she opened the latch and set her arm out in front of her. Usually Birds could not control others' namesakes, but this was different. The crow definitely knew. It didn't need any further encouragement, as it instantly fluttered over to her and perched on her arm. She then withdrew from the latch opening and sealed the cage back up again.

"It's time, Crow," Robin whispered. "Your human half has left the Eye. Time to return and be one."

The crow stared at her for a moment, its deep black eyes taking her in for the final time. Then with one soulful cry it beat its wings and left her arm. It rose higher and higher directly above Robin until it was a black spot over the camp. It then took off and headed directly for the Storm Wall, presumably to die and be reunited with its master.

After a few reflective moments, the Bird tribe dispersed.

Finch patted Robin's shoulder and also left her to her thoughts. But not Sparrow.

"What now?" Sparrow asked her friend. "I know that look. You're planning something."

"It wasn't for nothing," Robin answered. "Crow didn't die for nothing. It's that girl, you know."

"You said there was something strange about her. What did you mean?"

"It's not the end. I'm sure of it. Something's about to happen, and I want to be a part of it. For Crow."

Robin seemed confident in her statements, but Sparrow was unsure. Instead, a creeping hand of dread wormed its way over her. But Robin was her best friend. She would help her fellow Bird wherever it took them.

CHAPTER 13

Few dared to roam the open sands at night, but Deacon knew the paths unlike any other. His dirt bike weaved side to side with ease, his ability to navigate the dark desert unmatched.

Recent events involving the girl changed things. Deacon could see it the moment his son had carried her into the Pathfinder camp. He saw fear. He saw misunderstanding. He saw the old sentiments returning.

But he saw something else there, too. It started with Aiden, but it had bled out to the others.

He saw hope.

But at what cost would that hope demand? They had already guessed she'd come from beyond the Storm. How far would that path take them? Were they ready for what he knew was coming? They would need help from all the tribes if this would work. He would fulfill his promise to her. He would make the change.

Deacon's thoughts got pulled from him as the revving of

engines sounded. He glanced back over his shoulder and saw the very thing he'd hoped to avoid.

A large truck bore down on him, covered in spikes and armor, the obvious signs of a Dog vehicle.

Deacon swerved just out of the way as the truck almost smashed into him. Two Dogs were aboard, and the passenger took aim with his rifle.

The gun cracked and Deacon almost felt the bullet zip past his face. He increased his speed beyond the bike's limits and his traction became more unstable in the sandy paths. Deacon grimaced as he noticed the path itself narrow, their course heading toward some steep cliff edges. He tried to guide his bike away from the coming ledge, but the Dog truck zoomed up and in the way. Deacon saw no way out.

The rifle rang out again, and the bike's rear tire exploded. The resulting boom sent the bike and its rider through the air, up and over the nearest ledge and out of sight.

The Dogs hollered in triumph as they slowed the truck.

"Ted would want us to make sure he's a goner," the driver said, and he veered the truck to the ledge.

Deacon blinked his eyes open and cried in pain almost instantly. His shoulder didn't feel right. He also saw blood and sand caked all over his mangled legs, and the crumpled bike next to him. He struggled to move as he saw a small flame brewing into existence within the bike's engine parts. Then he smelled the fuel. He rolled over away from the bike and grunted in pain. He could barely move at all.

The flames grew higher.

He struggled onto his arms and shuffled himself inch by inch away from the bike. He glanced up at the ledge as he did, trying to spot the Dogs he knew would return.

The truck stopped, and the two Dogs got out. As they glanced down below, they could already see the faint orange glow.

And the flames grew higher still.

Despite his efforts, Deacon realized he hadn't gotten very far. He reached into his tunic and pulled the jade ring out. He pulled the chain from around his neck and curled the whole thing into the center of his gloved hand. He squeezed tight.

Aiden...

The passenger Dog fired his rifle a final time, directly into the growing mix of flame and fuel. The spark needed was lit, and a raging fireball exploded up from the ground. Even the two Dogs got knocked back to the ground from the explosion.

The fire consumed Deacon completely.

Once they returned to their feet, the Dogs whistled at the sight below. The bottom of the ledge had been destroyed. The explosion had altered the whole pit, the sandy surfaces had even been transformed to glass.

There was nothing left but melted and fused debris. Ashes descended to the ground in silent submission. And amid the destruction lay the charred corpse of Deacon, burned black and unrecognizable save for the size and shape of his body.

The Dogs laughed and returned to their truck. There'd be a party that night. They'd finally done it.

They'd finally killed Deacon.

CHAPTER 14

A calm and fresh morning greeted Aiden as he exited the tanker.

Hobbes was waiting eagerly outside. "Have a good night?"

"What?"

Hobbes couldn't hide the cheeky look that his face displayed. "Did you have a good night?"

"Uh, yeah. Why?" Aiden asked as they made their way into the camp.

"The word is out about your girlfriend."

"What?" Aiden glared. "She's not my girl-"

"She's causing a stir among the masses."

"What masses?" Aiden asked. "We're a tribe of barely a hundred people."

"A hundred and one if you keep at it," Hobbes grinned.

"Funny," Aiden groaned. "Just what are you getting at?"

Aiden paused then, as the sound of voices-many, many voices- echoed through the camp. The boys sped up and moved toward the commotion.

"Masses," Hobbes said. "As in more than just one tribe."

People from every tribe had gathered in the Pathfinder camp. Word had got around.

Bastion was present with a posse of Eagles, complete with purple cloaks and Eagle glyphs. Women of the Thorns were there, and Birds and even a handful of Dogs in all their leather-clad and inked glory. Everyone was asking of Nemo, but they could hear no specifics in the mass of questions.

Finally fed up, Isaiah climbed atop a truck and raised his hands to address the crowd. "Everyone, quiet! I'll try to answer your questions as best I can!"

"Is it true?" a Thorn woman asked. "She's not from the Eye?"

An elder Eagle next to Bastion called out. "We demand to see her! We demand you release her!"

"Released?" Isaiah scoffed. "She's not a prisoner! She's recovering here, that is all."

Aiden and Hobbes found Jonah and joined him.

"Should't Dad be talking?" Aiden asked his grandfather. "Where is he?"

"Hush," Jonah muttered. "Isaiah can handle this."

A tall, thin Bird tribe member raised his hand. "What do you mean 'recovering'? What happened?"

"We discovered the girl," Isaiah paused. "We found her in a crashed airplane."

A wave of shock passed over the crowd. They were speechless until the same Bird continued. "A plane from where?"

Aiden looked back to the tanker and saw Nemo peering out the small window next to the tanker entrance. Her eyes did not seem nervous or lost. Instead, he sensed determination in them.

Then, much to Hobbes's surprise, Aiden leaped atop the truck next to Isaiah. "From beyond the Storm!"

Silence followed.

"Come on," he continued. "We're all thinking it. Where else?"

Isaiah leaned class and whispered. "What do you think you're doing?"

"She can't answer our questions," Aiden said, unhindered. "Nemo doesn't speak our language. That leaves only one answer. She came from beyond the Storm!"

"That's not true," Bastion spoke. "There is nothing beyond the Storm! Only ruin!"

"According to whom?" Aiden asked.

"According to the word of the Storm!" Bastion declared.

"She's a heathen!" the elder Eagle added. "She is a bringer of false hope to all who listen to her!"

Another Thorn woman spoke. "Airplanes are a myth in books. They don't exist anymore!"

They then threw words and insults around through the tribes, reverting the people back into a mass of squawking babble.

Isaiah growled at Aiden. "This situation is fragile enough without you-"

"You think I want to believe it?" Aiden cut in. "All I know is the Eye. All any of us know is the Eye. A world outside the Storm can't be real. How could it? But she is real. We don't have a choice."

Hobbes, though still on the ground, reached up and tugged on Aiden's pant leg. "Guys?"

"You're causing a riot!" Isaiah said. "And all for what is probably some fairy tale."

Hobbes kept tugging. "Guys? Seriously, look!"

They finally looked down to Hobbes and saw he was pointing. They followed his gaze to a nearby path at the camp's perimeter.

The morning sun silhouetted a mysterious figure which stood stoic at the entrance to the camp. As additional tribesmen noticed also, the noise faded. Soon the crowd became silent, and the figure made its approach.

"A Stormwalker," Isaiah whispered in awe.

Rags, cloak, armor and goggles covered the Stormwalker's appearance. Bandages wrapped his body and arms, neck, not a single inch of skin exposed. He had a rifle strapped to his back, and a large curved blade sheathed in his belt. The stranger had a look perfectly adapted to nomadic life within the Storm.

As he made his approach through the crowd he walked calmly, distinctly, never taking his goggle-tinted gaze off the two atop the truck. When he reached the truck, the Stormwalker turned around to face the crowd, who were all gawking in surprise. He noted the few children present, many of whom carried little Stormwalker dolls with them.

The Stormwalker stared. "You fight among each other while hope sits in this very camp."

Isaiah broke the quiet reverence of the seldom-seen figure. "What brings you here, Stormwalker?"

Instead of speaking, the Stormwalker pointed at the tanker.

"What of her?" Aiden asked.

"Are you not yet ready?" the Stormwalker asked.

Isaiah tried to hide his anxiety. "Ready for what?"

"To leave," the Stormwalker answered, his motive impossible to tell behind his goggles and bandages.

The tribes were once again struck silent.

"You can't be serious," Bastion finally declared. "Why would we leave?"

"If you stay, you will die," the Stormwalker stated.

"What's it talking about?" a Thorn woman asked.

Jonah stepped forward then. "Our charts show the Storm will reach the Storm in a few months. This time next cycle we'll be drowning."

Aiden recognized the surprise of the tribes at the news. "It's true. I've seen the charts. The Storm moves east more every cycle. Soon we'll be trapped."

Jonah regarded the Stormwalker. "You knew this."

The Stormwalker nodded.

Isaiah shook his head. "And we're just supposed to believe this thing? Just like that? How do we trust it to get us through?"

"I walk the Storm," the Stormwalker answered. "Its secrets are more than you can imagine, and I know them all."

"No! You're wrong!" Bastion declared. "There is only the Storm! We cannot follow this thing into the unknown of the Storm! It's suicide! It's sacrilege!"

"Decide!" the Stormwalker demanded.

Moments passed between the tribes. Isaiah kept shaking his head, but Jonah decided. He approached the Stormwalker, hobbling on his cane.

"I cannot speak for the other tribes," Jonah said. "But I believe you. The Pathfinders will follow. Show us the way."

The Stormwalker nodded. "In two days the Eye will pass over the ruins of the Stone Man. It is there the travelers will meet me. But know this. Only a handful of you may go. The journey will be long. Dangerous. I can watch over only a few."

"We understand," Jonah muttered.

The Stormwalker abruptly turned to leave, but paused as the thrum of an engine became known. Everyone watched as a Pathfinder scout riding a dirt bike and pulling a sled drove into camp and stopped right in front of Jonah. He whispered to Jonah as the Stormwalker waited. Jonah glanced at the sled, and the bundle wrapped upon it.

"I'm telling you this is blasphemy," Bastion yelled to the Stormwalker. "None of the other tribes will follow this fool!"

Jonah stared at the Stormwalker for a moment. Then, "We'll do as you say, Stormwalker. We will meet you there."

The Stormwalker nodded and left, not regarding anyone else as it passed.

"We are done here," Jonah told the tribes. "If you choose to join us, return next moon."

The tribes reluctantly trickled away, and Aiden jumped back down to ground level. He then almost shook as Jonah clasped his shoulder.

He could see it in his grandfather's eyes. "Tell me."

Jonah shook his head. "Aiden, I'm so sorry."

The sun had set, and the wind had waned. The Pathfinders gathered around a large pile of wood, Deacon's wrapped body rested atop the mound.

Aiden held a burning torch, and resting it against the base of the pyre, set the kindling ablaze. Small at first, the fire spread and grew, and as Aiden backed away, he watched the pyre become consumed in flame.

"The Eye is to blame," Jonah muttered as Aiden returned to him. "It was the Dogs, surely. But the Storm swallows us all. We can never choose when it happens."

Aiden said nothing. He did not fight back the tears that formed. Nemo stood at Aiden's other side, and she watched him intently. As she saw the tears, she took his hand in hers and gave a reassuring squeeze. It caused Aiden to draw his gaze from the fire onto her. She smiled at him, and he found himself surprisingly comforted. He smiled back, and as they looked back to the fire together, he made his decision.

"Maybe for once," Aiden finally said, "maybe this time we can choose."

Nemo gave his hand another squeeze.

As they stood atop a distant hillside, Jorus, Bastion and a handful of Eagles watched the funeral fire. Bastion, as usual, stood with his arms crossed. Jorus, however, pressed his palms together and bowed his head, his purple cloak and hood obscuring him. He mumbled a few words and then raised his head again. The far off fire glinted in his eyes, and a sinister grin slowly formed.

CHAPTER 15

The next morning Hobbes found Aiden sitting at a table in the food area. He was alone, staring at his untouched breakfast.

"You okay?" Hobbes asked his friend.

"Everyone in the Eye has lost someone, Hobbes," Aiden muttered. "I'll manage."

Hobbes took a seat next to Aiden. "You still have Jonah. And look, when I lost my folks it didn't take long to realize how many people I still had all around me."

Aiden glanced around at the Pathfinders, who bustled about. They were people he'd known his whole life. They were people he suddenly found the desire to fight for.

"Maybe you're right," Aiden admitted. "After yesterday, this tribe needs help more than ever."

"Who is this guy? What happened to my friend Aiden?" Hobbes asked with a smirk. "What happened to messing around at the market? Trouble? Fun? Girls?"

"Something has to change, Hobbes."

83

"This... journey," Hobbes nodded. "Deacon was gonna lead... but he's gone now. I'm sorry."

Aiden shook his head. "Hobbes, I'm gonna lead this mission."

Hobbes stared, shoulders drooped, mouth agape, as Aiden stood and walked away. Eventually he collected himself and caught up to his friend, who had walked to a large water tank and filled a thermos.

"So you're gonna follow the Stormwalker? And just trust what he... it... whatever he has to say? We only hear stories of these people our whole lives and now one just shows up and we all just bow down to him?"

Aiden pointed at the far-off Storm Wall, the swirling and raging of it clear. "Do you walk around in that?"

Hobbes just stuttered.

"Face it," Aiden continued. "The Stormwalkers are our best hope of getting through there."

"Well, it's hard to trust someone who has no face," Hobbes grunted.

Just then, Jonah hobbled around the corner of the water tank, his gait relying on his cane with every step. "You cannot see the wind, yet you trust it to steer you where you need."

Aiden handed Jonah his thermos of water. "What do you think of all this?"

Jonah took a long, refreshing drink and then sighed a breath of relief. "I say we trust him."

"But we know nothing about them," Hobbes said.

"True," Jonah admitted. "But the Stormwalker trusted us enough to come and talk to us face to face."

"Well, face to mask," Hobbes argued.

"But what about the tribe?" Aiden asked. "Dad's gone... and... I..."

"This is for the tribe," Jonah replied. "Besides, I led this tribe for thirty years before your father, remember? And like you, your mother didn't make it easy. I can handle it until you return with an answer."

"Are you sure? I ask myself if this is what Dad would want me to do."

"Deacon lived a complicated life," Jonah admitted. "But I know something for sure. He knew that one day you would be a leader. So go. Lead us a way out of this forsaken Storm, eh?"

Aiden decided then and nodded.

A smaller but still impressive crowd of all the tribes returned later that evening. Provisions were packed, and an old truck prepared. The journey was ready to begin.

Aiden and Jonah stood amidst the crowd, Aiden dressed in a multi-layered outfit with gear to face the Storm.

"Are you ready?" Jonah asked his grandson.

"As ready as I'm gonna be," Aiden replied.

Nemo and Hobbes approached them, similarly dressed for the expedition.

"Tá sé am," Nemo said as she tightened a glove.

"Aiden, I'm coming with you," Hobbes said with defiance. "Nothing you can say to stop me. Nope, don't even try to talk me out of this. Someone's gotta watch out for you. Someone who can yell 'Look out!' in your own language."

Aiden smirked. "I wouldn't have it any other way."

Jonah turned to the crowd. "I see many eager faces from the tribes! If any have chosen to, now is the time to step forward."

Robin was the first to step forward. It was something she knew she had to do, and she would do so in Crow's honor.

Directly behind her stood her two biggest supporters, Finch and Sparrow. They also stepped forward.

Next stepped Larina. She confidently marched toward the front of the crowd, raising her spear in salute. The other Thorn women present called their support to her. She spotted Hobbes and smirked, an expression which Hobbes couldn't help but return.

Aiden scanned the crowd. "Is that everyone?"

Last, Creed uncrossed his arms and swaggered forward to join the others. The older man grinned at Aiden. "I guess someone capable had better watch out for you, boy."

Aiden nodded his gratitude to his fellow Pathfinder.

Jonah patted Aiden's back. "I'm proud of you, Aiden. Despite everything, Deacon would be too."

"Lead the way, buddy," Hobbes said.

Aiden hugged Jonah, then nodded and turned to the crowd. Nemo nodded to him, and he took a breath. "This journey will prove once and for all what our future will hold. I know there is doubt. But if we can find safe land beyond the Storm, all of this will be worth it. This will be a dangerous journey, but where others have failed out there, we will succeed. Let us knock at the Storm's door and see what answers!"

Great cheering erupted as the group headed out.

"Dream free!" Jonah called. "All of you!"

Creed hopped into the truck, which had been loaded with most of their supplies. He drove it slowly as the others walked on each side.

As they walked, Nemo turned to Aiden. "Aiden, Tá tá tú ag déanamh an rud ceart. Feicfidh tú a fheiceáil."

Hobbes just shrugged, but Aiden smiled at her.

The remaining tribe members waved and said their goodbyes as the travelers passed. No one was sure when, or if, they would see each other again, or what the future, for all of them, would hold.

As the cool night settled in, most of the Dog tribe sat around the fires and tables that littered their camp. They shouted, drank, and were loud and obnoxious to each other.

As Ted and Vic sat outside Ted's camper, Ted frantically scrubbed himself down in a large water trough.

"Teddy," Vic said. "No matter how hard you scrub, that smell ain't going anywhere."

"What would you know?" Ted growled. "Have you smelled yourself lately?"

"You'll use all the camp's water supply before you smell better."

"Then I'll take the damn Birds' water!" Ted shouted. "It's their fault I smell like ancient garbage!"

"You *did* try to kill them, Teddy."

"Try? You're the one who got to have all the fun!" Ted replied. "And stop calling me Teddy! I'm sick of you disrespecting me and challenging my lead."

"I'm looking out for-"

"Shut up, Vic!" Ted interrupted. "Just stop, or I'll leave your ass in the Storm next time we-"

A commotion broke Ted's attention at the camp's perimeter. Illuminated between two fire pits, a procession of Eagle priests entered the camp. In the center of them walked Jorus. Most of the Dogs present looked anxious that there were Eagles in the camp. Neither Ted nor Vic bothered to stand as Jorus approached.

"Theodore," Jorus greeted.

"What?" Ted asked. "What could you want bad enough to actually show your old face around my camp?"

The other Dogs crowded in and stared menacingly, eager to fight. But Jorus wasn't phased.

"I trust our arrangement is still valid?" the elder Eagle asked.

Ted smirked and signaled for the Dogs to back off. They did so, reluctantly.

"I have a job for you," Jorus continued.

Finally, Ted stood and faced Jorus at eye level.

"Another job, huh?" Ted said. "What, like the last one? It was a disaster! You have any idea how long they trapped us in that bunker? We're not your pets, Jorus. Walking into my tribe takes balls, I'll give you that. But you expect too much."

"Very well," Jorus said. "If you are tired of being paid for your work, tired of reaping the rewards of our joint venture, then I'm sure our spare gas and food can be used elsewhere."

"We don't need you. We have-"

"You have nothing!" Jorus broke his calm. "You don't even try to survive on your own! All you do is take, take, take."

"What's wrong with that?"

Jorus regained his composure. "Nothing, if kept in check. The tribes of the Eye are cattle. I just want you to herd them for me, without the attitude please. My flock will need strong shepherds, Theodore. You can be such a shepherd, if you want to be."

"Cut to it, Jorus," Vic sighed. "What's the job?"

Ted glared at his brother for what he saw as yet another act of belittling his leadership. He would pay for that later.

"You must know of this expedition that has unfolded," Jorus replied.

"Through the Storm, yeah," Ted said. "Stupid plan. And I hear Deacon... dropped out."

The other Dogs laughed.

Jorus shook his head. "I thought this nonsense would die with Deacon. But it seems to have moved ahead with his own son in charge."

"What do I care?" Ted scoffed. "Let them wander off and die in the Storm. More room for us in the Eye."

Jorus then sniffed the air. "What is that awful smell? Is it the pit they locked you in? Or is that the smell of failure, at the hands of children, no less?"

Ted turned crimson.

Jorus didn't care. "You can get your payback. I want you to stop this mission. I want to make it so no one ever questions their place in the Eye ever again. I want you to make them pay. And I want you to enjoy doing it."

Hearing this, Ted calmed. The red faded, and instead of answering Jorus, he turned to his Dogs. "Seems the other tribes are taking an unscheduled Walk! They say they are boldly trekking out through the Storm for a reason. Know what I say? I say they're running away! Well, are we gonna let them?"

The Dogs chanted and roared a resounding no.

"They think they can escape us?" Ted continued. "Well, it's not the Storm they need to fear out there! It's us! They are vermin and we are the Dogs!"

More cheering.

Jorus smiled and left without saying anymore, flanked by his priests.

"Teddy what are we doing?" Vic asked. "Why are we always answering to him?"

"As long as they pay, we play," Ted said.

"But we are our own tribe. Not-"

"Jorus can bark his orders and feed us his lies all he wants. He'll be sorry when the day comes that the Dogs bite back!"

Ted joined the Dogs in their cheering. They gathered their weapons and mounted their bikes and vehicles.

Vic did not agree. Then he realized they had left him alone before he hopped aboard a passing truck.

He had a bad feeling about the battle to come.

CHAPTER 16

The expedition had made good ground, the journey to the Storm Wall well on its way. After setting up camp for the night, Nemo retired to her tent. Everyone else sat around the fire, the discussion illuminated by the flame.

"So then the lizard leaps out at him," Hobbes said, "and Aiden tumbles headfirst down the steep dune! Took him an hour to climb back up."

Everyone laughed, save for Aiden and Creed.

"I swear," Hobbes continued, "he must have weighed five times as much with all that sand down his pants."

"Yeah, yeah. Laugh it up," Aiden said. "Should I tell everyone about your mishap what that Thorn girl? What was her name, Daisy?"

Larina perked up at the mention of it. "And what mishap would that be?"

"Well," Aiden replied, "a couple cycles ago, Hobbes here had himself a late night meet up with this Thorn girl. Only he didn't know yet that in Thorn custom, even a simple kiss is a proposal."

"That was you?" Larina demanded of Hobbes. "You're the reason our tribes didn't speak for weeks!"

"How was I supposed to know?" Hobbes explained. "According to Daisy we're still engaged."

Again, almost everyone laughed. But not Creed. "You all think the Stormwalker will be there waiting for us?"

The mood shifted then.

"How many you think are out there?" Hobbes asked no one in particular. "You know, like her?"

Creed nodded. "If she really is from out there somewhere, then maybe there are a lot more. Where is she, anyway?"

"Nemo?" Aiden said. "In her tent. Maybe I should check on her."

"Yeah, maybe you should," Creed said. "Not like this whole mission relies on her or anything."

"We'll handle things out here," Hobbes smirked. "Have a good night, friend!"

Aiden shook his head as he moved to Nemo's tent. Grasping the zipper, he poked his head in the entrance. "I thought I'd check in on-"

He paused at the sight before him. Nemo had her face buried in books, oblivious to his arrival.

Aiden crawled inside. "You're reading?"

She finally popped her head up to look at him. She smiled as she patted the ground next to her. "Come. Sit."

Aiden did so, then did a double take. "Wait, so you talk now? Our language, I mean?"

She nodded. "I learn."

"I have so much to ask you!" Aiden suddenly blurted out. "Did you really fly that plane? From where? Are there more people out there? Where do we go to get there?"

Nemo just stared and blinked.

"Right. Right," Aiden realized. "Slow down, Aiden. Okay. So where did you fly the plane from?"

He motioned with his hand as he stuck his pinky finger and thumb outward, mimicking the shape of an aircraft with wings.

"Fly. Yes," Nemo said.

"But from where? How many of you are there?"

She just stared.

He got an idea. He pointed at her. "You. One."

She nodded.

He pointed at her and himself. "You and me. Two."

She nodded.

He pointed to her again. "How many of you, out there?"

She watched him for some time, and he decided she just did not understand.

But then, finally, her warm gaze sunk slightly. "Few."

Aiden nodded. "So, how did you get here? Where from?"

She stared at him for a time and concentrated. But it was no use. Soon she just sighed. "No remember."

Aiden was disappointed, but not surprised. She must have taken a hard knock to the head in that crash. "It'll come in time, I'm sure." Then he prepared himself for the one question he just had to know. He leaned closer. "What is your name?"

She almost answered. In the last moment, however, something went through her mind, Aiden could tell.

She just nodded. "Nemo."

"Okay," Aiden sighed. "Maybe you'll understand soon. For now, Nemo it is."

"Aiden."

"Yes, I'm Aiden."

Nemo abruptly grabbed his hand in hers and squeezed

playfully. She continued to hold on, well into the awkwardness Aiden began to feel.

"Aiden and Nemo," she smiled.

Aiden couldn't help but smile too. Then the two former strangers, now fast growing friends, looked over the various books and charts the group had brought with them. Aiden did his best to impress words on her to learn, while Nemo did her best to understand and grow along with him. The two studied, talked, laughed and enjoyed one another's company, well into the depths of the night.

CHAPTER 17

The Storm Wall grew closer, but the group still had far to go before reaching the outer limits of the Eye and taking the plunge into the wilds of the storm itself.

The winds had increased and caused everyone to wear goggles, otherwise they'd get blinded in the growing chaos.

Aiden drove the truck, with Nemo seated in the passenger seat. She kept glancing at him and smiling, then looking off into the distance, where a large shape gradually became plain within the swirling distance.

"Those must be the ruins the Stormwalker spoke of," Aiden said. "The Stone Man."

Hobbes walked outside with Creed while Robin, Sparrow, Finch and Larina rode in the back of the truck. As they moved along, Robin rummaged through her bag and pulled out a battered toy unicorn. Its paint had mostly faded and its fibrous mane barely remained.

Creed noticed her handling the unicorn. "What's with the toy?"

Robin turned and placed the unicorn upon the roof of the truck cab.

"When I was a child, there was a book I learned to read with. It was about these magical creatures called unicorns," Robin explained as she fastened the toy in place with a bit of wire. "Like the horses the Thorns use, but these horses had these horns on their heads. I always thought they were just legends, you know, in books. Until I found this. Someone made this with their own hands. Someone must have seen one!"

"A horse with a horn," Creed scoffed. "What's the big deal?"

"Unicorns were magic, Creed," Robin replied, a little hurt. "Magic means luck. This is my lucky unicorn. I figure we can use all the luck we can get."

As if on cue, a roar of engines sounded. As the group looked to their rear, they saw an approaching wave of vehicles, mostly bikes but also a few other cars. Ted rode one bike, Vic following closely behind. They were under attack!

"Dogs!" Robin screamed.

Hobbes quickly raised his rifle and took aim, firing at the oncoming Dogs. Robin, Finch, and Sparrow followed with their own handguns right after.

Inside the truck, Aiden handed Nemo a handgun. "I hope you know how to use this."

Nemo answered by cocking the gun and leaping outside. Aiden followed close behind.

The group and the Dogs exchanged gunfire.

"Take them down, boys!" Ted ordered from behind the firing line. "Make them pay for trapping us in that bunker. They ain't getting another step further!"

The Dogs obeyed. The expedition members took cover

behind the opposite side of their truck and attempted to return fire. However, the dust in the growing winds swirled ever thicker, and visibility got poorer.

It was the same for the Dogs though, and as they fired their pot shots at their trapped targets, they did not notice the figure amidst them in the dusty confusion. A Dog went down, followed by another. A third got stabbed where he stood. Their attacker was unseen, and they dropped like flies without a sound.

Soon, Aiden took notice of the dwindling rate of fire coming from their attackers. Risking a peek around the corner of the truck, he could tell that something had happened. He could tell the number of Dogs had drastically diminished.

"Okay!" Aiden called to the group. "Charge them!"

The group then emerged from their cover and charged into the dusty fray, firing at what targets they saw.

As Robin ran, she did not see the large mass of a figure looming before her. She collided with him, and falling back, looked up into the face of Vic. He had his gun trained on her, but as he got a look at his target, a young woman not even a quarter his size, he faltered.

Instead, he sighed, and with his other hand, offered to help her up. She hesitated, then relented and gave him her hand. He hoisted her up, nodded, and turned away.

A Dog car screeched into view then. The driver took notice of Robin, and, revving the car's engine, barreled down upon her.

Vic saw what was about to happen and turned back to Robin. He charged and tackled her off her feet just out of the way of the oncoming car, the two of them thrown into the sand.

The car continued on blindly and smashed directly into the group's only truck, totaling both.

Robin looked from their wrecked truck to Vic, surprised at who it was that'd just saved her.

Vic said nothing, instead opting to hoist his large frame out of the sand run back into the conflict.

Standing at his bike, Ted saw the whole scene unfold ahead. He roared in anger, and as she spotted Aiden sprinting across the battlefield, he leveled his gun on the young man.

A booted foot struck him in the side. Ted went down, then rolled, allowing him to end back on his feet. He clutched at his rib cage and spun to face his attacker.

It was Nemo. She stood in a defensive stance, hands up and ready.

Ted couldn't believe what he was seeing. The little twerp dared to confront him, *him*, directly? He laughed.

He stopped laughing when Nemo rushed toward him. She was much quicker than he'd expected and was on him in an instant. She jumped and delivered another kick, but he got his arms up in time. Still, he felt the power behind her strike, and felt his forearm dare to break under the strain. She then came at him with repeated palm strikes, some making their way through his defenses to strike his chest and face.

She pulled her gun from her belt, but as she brought it to bear on him, he swatted it from her hand. He could see on her face though that she didn't seem to care. Instead, she charged again with more hand strikes.

Ted was being pummeled, but finally he used his size to swing his arms and hit her like a falling tree. Nemo went down, and as she crawled in the sand, he found her discarded gun.

He took aim, only to get blocked when another Dog landed

at his feet. Ted turned to face the goggled and wrapped visage of the Stormwalker. The bandaged nomad had a curved blade in hand.

Ted stared at the tall, silent figure, then whipped the gun to bear on him. "Stormwalker!"

The Stormwalker stood stoic.

"The knife!" Ted demanded. "Throw it away!"

Instead, the Stormwalker slowly raised his hands as if in surrender. His rags and bindings around his arms whipped in the wind. Ted lowered the gun just slightly, and that was the moment the Stormwalker needed. Suddenly Onyx chucked the knife out to the side, nowhere near Ted. The sudden action caused Ted to raise the gun again, but he laughed when he saw the blade fly off. He continued to laugh while the blade, spinning in the wind like a propeller, boomeranged back around Ted and sunk itself into his arm.

Ted dropped the gun and gave out a great howl of pain. He retreated, and as he looked back, saw the Stormwalker had already vanished. Only Nemo remained as Aiden arrived, helping her up.

The Dogs regathered.

Aiden and Nemo watched the Dogs as a forceful hand gripped his shoulder and whipped him around to face its owner.

"Stormwalker," Aiden greeted the nomad.

"The Storm is upon us!" the Stormwalker advised over the growing roar of the wind. "We cannot continue to fight like this. The Stone Man is to the east!"

Aiden nodded, calling out to the others, who had also regathered. "Fall back! To the ruins!"

The Dogs returned to their vehicles. As Vic reached the

tailgate of one truck, he found his brother sitting in the back clutching, clutching at his wounded arm. Vic climbed in.

"Your arm," Vic noticed.

"Yeah, my goddamn arm!" Ted shouted. "And where were you, to watch my back?"

"I was-"

"You saved that girl! The people we're supposed to be stopping!"

"She was just a girl."

"And you're just a waste of space!"

Ted suddenly kicked Vic in the chest, which launched him over the side of the truck and into the sand. Vic hit the ground hard as the truck departed.

"Have fun with your new friends!" Ted called as they rode out.

Vic was alone.

The Storm only got worse. Barely able to even breathe in the increasingly dusty winds, the group arrived at their destination; the Stone Man ruins. They had believed the structure to be an ancient shrine. It was a singular structure that appeared to have once had multiple pillars lined at the entrance, but the pillars themselves had long ago toppled and broken to the ground. The structures ceiling had also collapsed, leaving the interior prone to the outside elements. Within was a singular room where a very large, generations-old statue of a bearded man, sitting calmly, stared outward. Most of the wording on the nearby murals had worn off long ago, but they could make a few letters out; ABR AM L NCO N

They made their way inside. As they entered the ruins, nobody noticed the strange thing clinging to the wall above. It hid its form in cloak and shadow. As the group entered, it skittered up and away, reptilian-like in its movements. Then it was gone.

Inside, the group finally had time to rest. But not Hobbes. Instead, he slammed his fist on a wall.

"Well, that's just great!" he yelled. "We left everything behind! There's no way we can go back for it now!"

"The Dogs will surely take everything," Larina agreed.

"Then we make do with what we have," the Stormwalker said.

"We have no supplies now!" Hobbes replied. "How will we survive?"

"The Storm will provide."

"Oh, yes, thanks Mr. Stormwalker. How the hell-"

"Hobbes!" Aiden burst out. "Stop."

"What?"

"You're not helping," Aiden sighed. "Okay, everyone. Yes, we're low on supplies. But we're not done yet. We can still do this."

"Stormwalker," Larina said to the stranger, "First, what do we call you? You don't just go by Stormwalker, do you?"

The Stormwalker hesitated for a moment, glancing at Aiden. But a moment later the ragged nomad spoke. "I am called Onyx. I shall be your guide. This is my task."

Hobbes laughed. "Well, good job so far."

"Ignore him," Aiden said. "We all thank you for your help back there."

Onyx could see the reluctant agreement on the other's faces, but he nodded anyway.

"I mean it," Aiden continued. "Your people might be our salv-"

Onyx suddenly whipped his rifle up, aiming at the room's

entrance. At that moment Vic emerged from the Storm, coughing and sputtering as he stumbled into the middle of the room.

"A Dog!" Larina cried.

Creed, Aiden and Hobbes rushed to pile on him and hold him to the floor.

"Get off!" Vic coughed. "Get off me!"

"No, wait!" Robin said. "He helped me back there."

Onyx cocked his rifle.

"He saved me from the other Dogs!" she pleaded.

"Why would he do that?" Hobbes asked. "They're trying to kill us!"

"Well, he did," she replied.

Aiden took a chance and stood up off Vic. "Why are you trying to stop us?"

"I don't care what you do," Vic replied, still restrained by Hobbes and Creed. "I was just helping my brother."

Onyx lowered his rifle. "The brother who left you behind."

"Yeah, that one."

Aiden nodded, and Creed and Hobbes eased off. Vic stood shakily.

"You helped me," Robin said to Vic.

"Didn't seem right not to," Vic muttered.

"But you're a Dog," Hobbes said, confused. "Since when have you ever helped another tribe?"

Vic seethed. "You other tribes are the ones who call us that, you know! There was a time they called something else. We were the Axles, and we were damn proud of it! But the other tribes just used us again and again until we said no more. After that, the tribes treated us like dogs, so Dogs are what we became. Especially the Eagles, but you all do it too."

Larina didn't care. "You tried to kill us. Forgive me for not showing much sympathy here."

Onyx slung his rifle back over his shoulder. "Enough. Time to choose. What shall you do with him?"

Creed shook his head. "Another mouth to feed."

"Another mouth to feed?" Hobbes asked. "You mean this trip is still happening? We lost everything!"

The Stormwalker was silent for a moment, and then, "Choose."

"The Dogs tried to kill us," Larina said again. "All I gotta say."

Robin approached Aiden. "He saved my life. That must count for something?"

Aiden regarded Vic. Despite the man's size, he seemed small now, abandoned by his brethren. Aiden pitied him.

"Either you leave right now and go into the Storm," Aiden declared, "or you come with us. You help us. You be part of something that's bigger than the Dogs or the Eagles or any of us."

Vic sighed. "I been abandoned. I got no tribe now, anyway."

"Out here, we are our own tribe," Aiden said. "No Pathfinders. No Dogs. No nothing. It's just us. Time to act like it. You want in or are we done here?"

Aiden reached out his hand. After a few moments Vic took it and shook, nodding. Robin smiled.

"Good, great," Hobbes muttered. "We can all die together. Hooray."

"Aiden," Creed spoke up, "remember, we have no supplies. No food. All we have is what's on our backs. And what the Stormwalker provides. Are we really gonna remain in his debt like that?"

"It's not about debt," Aiden reasoned. "We follow him. End of story. You don't like it, you can leave."

"Nah, kid. I think your dad would'a wanted me to keep an eye on you," Creed replied. "I'm in this to the end. I just got a feeling that end ain't too far off."

Later, Aiden and Nemo took it upon themselves to scout further into the ruins while the others took stock of their remaining supplies. The Stone Man ruins expanded further in with side rooms and hallways beyond the main statue area.

They soon discovered other ancient works of art, paintings and murals mostly, that lined the forgotten halls. It was in front of these weathered murals that Nemo took hold of Aiden's arm, stopping him.

"Glad you're okay," she said.

Aiden grinned. "I'm fine. I've gotten out of some bad fights, but that one was rough."

"Why you call them Dogs?"

Aiden thought about it. "I guess it's just what we've always known them by. They're savage, Nemo."

"Like Stormwalker?"

"No, not really. I don't think so. See, the Dogs have never cared about the other tribes. They raid and just take everything. They don't care who they kill."

Nemo seemed confused. "You kill Dogs to save me. You savage too?"

"No. I... I mean..."

"Other tribes take all they can, yes?"

"Yes, but..."

"But they not savage?"

"I know. It's not fair. Life in the Eye isn't fair. We're trapped."

"But I help. I free you."

"I hope so. As soon as you start leading the way."

She shook her head. "Not yet. Don't know where we are. Where come from."

"That's Onyx's job. He'll lead us through the Storm until you are familiar enough to lead us to your home. Yes?"

"Yes."

"I think this will work, Nemo. I really think we can change things. Thank you."

She took his hand in hers then, and placed his palm firmly against her chest, directly over her heart. She then pulled her own hand away, leaving his against her.

He stayed.

"Heart," she said.

"Heartbeat, yeah," Aiden agreed, finding himself looking in her eyes. Her eyes were deep, the color seeming to go on forever. There was a glint of something too, something that he felt drawn toward. He could not look away.

"Heart," she repeated, returning the look. As their eyes locked on each other, they couldn't deny the pull.

Somewhere along the way, a change had happened. Aiden knew it. He knew she knew it too. As he watched the mysterious girl, he knew she wasn't just the mission anymore. She had become so much more.

He also realized a devastating idea, the realization that not getting to see this girl every day would break him. So he let his hand drop back down, abandoning her longing heartbeat.

"I won't be around forever," Aiden sighed. "Once we get through, once we succeed, I'll have to return to the Pathfinders."

"Return," Nemo repeated.

"Back home."

Nemo once again gently took his hand and placed it over her heart. She pressed harder.

"Home," she declared.

He kissed her then.

When he finally drew away, they stared at each other, not just as two people thrown together in a crazy plan to save lives, but as two young people who could see, truly see, the human being in front of them. Feel that person. Know that person. It was a warm knowing, and in that moment Aiden realized he had felt it from those first moments when he pulled her from the plane.

She took his face in her hands then and drew him back to her. Their lips met, and she returned the kiss she could not deny.

He knew in that moment that it was meant to be.

While the others rested and went over their few remaining supplies, Finch sat at the ruins' entrance, tending to a wound on his arm from the fight. As he did so, he scanned the horizon beyond. He then noticed a movement in the distance, and recognizing what it was, he froze.

"Oh, hell," Finch gulped.

Onyx and Hobbes took stock of the few weapons and food that remained. Aiden rested against a wall, Nemo next to him, her head resting on his shoulder. He had just started falling asleep when Finch rushed in upon them, ripping him back to waking.

"We got company!" Finch cried.

"The Dogs must have doubled back on us!" Aiden said as he stood. "Get ready. Onyx, stay out of sight. Be our sniper and surprise them."

The Stormwalker nodded and disappeared into the ruins' shadows. As they could hear movement from outside the entrance, everyone else raised their weapons, ready for a final battle with the Dogs. But it wasn't the Dogs who entered the room.

Instead, Bastion appeared, accompanied by two Eagle guards. He glanced at each person's shocked face.

"Hello," Bastion grinned.

CHAPTER 18

5 YEARS PRIOR

The market bustled with activity. Vendors and customers moved about their business, and few took notice of the young woman, Mira, who casually strolled along the booths. She hummed a low tune to herself, lost in warm thoughts. Vendors smiled at her as she scanned over them, her face a friendly one to their daily schedules.

Mira stopped at a kiosk that sold different plants and flowers grown in vehicles or found out in the Eye. Her gaze passed over the myriad of colors and types of plants for sale, and she took notice of the different ways plants had to adapt to exist in the Storm.

"Pretty, aren't they?" a voice familiar to her said from behind. Mira turned to see Bastion, a much calmer and gracious version of him, watching her. There wasn't a single scar present on his body.

Mira smiled. "They are. Wish I had some of my own."

"Well, you're in luck," Bastion replied as he reached behind himself and brought out a flower intended for her. The flower was a bright orange color, with deep crimson stripes that etched along its bulb. "From the wastelands, to my Mira."

    Mira took the flower and smelled it. It smelled of honey and ginger.

    "I found it on the last raid," he continued. "It was all alone. A sole beauty amidst the chaos."

    "Okay," Mira chuckled. "Don't overdo it."

    "I can't help it," Bastion smiled as the two continued to walk through the market. "I'm just anxious. Two days from now we'll be married. We'll be on our way to a new future."

    "A future together," she added, taking his hand in her free hand.

    "That reminds me. Jorus said he had to speak with me, and soon. I think it's finally happening. We're gonna be set."

    "You've worked hard for it. I'm sure Lord Jorus has noticed. He couldn't ask for a more loyal Eagle. That old fool would be lucky to have you as his apprentice."

    Bastion glanced around them, hoping none had heard her. "Careful, Mira. Please don't insult Jorus's name, especially in public. I'm the one who'll be lucky to even get to speak with him."

    Mira stared ahead, reluctant to go on.

    "Mira? What is it?"

    She glanced at the kiosk nearest to them, a vendor selling many odds and ends, including Stormwalker dolls. She looked back to her future husband.

    "I know my working towards an apprenticeship with Jorus has never sat well with you," Bastion continued. "Please, I need your support."

    Finally, she sighed. "It's not the work. It's the man."

"What do you mean?"

"Jorus isn't the man you think he is. He's put on this false face for people to look up to. To follow. I've never believed it."

"Don't say those things," Bastion pleaded. "Mira, you're bordering on blasphemy."

"Why? Because the all-powerful Jorus declares it so?"

"If I get this apprenticeship, we'll be set for life. Don't you see that?"

"Don't you see the game he's playing? Don't you see that you'll just be another of his pawns?"

"What are you talking about? I get that you're not fond of the man. In time, I think you'll warm to him though. He'll help us out so much."

She smiled warmly. "You're not even listening. It's okay. I realize now that you may be too far gone."

Bastion shook his head. "I don't understand."

"I love you, Bastion. So much so I'm willing to put myself at risk now, for you. To help you…"

"You're not making any sense."

"Do you trust me?" she asked abruptly.

"What? Why?"

"Do you trust me?"

Bastion blinked at her, unsure of what any of it meant. Then, finally, "Yes. I'll always trust you."

She nodded. "Okay then."

Mira turned to the nearby booth.

"Ah, Mira," the booth vendor, an old man with a warm smile, greeted. "A sight for sore eyes. Your day going well?"

"Lovely," Mira replied. She hooked her arm around Bastion's. "This is Bastion. We'll be married in two days. He's working towards an apprenticeship with Jorus."

The vendor regarded Bastion a moment.

"Though he could use some air," she continued. "Too much time studying old, moldy books in his tent."

After a moment, the old vendor let out a quiet laugh. "Well, nothing wrong with that, eh? Means he's a clever one, yes?"

Bastion just shrugged, perplexed by the conversation.

"See anything special?" Mira asked Bastion.

Still unsure, Bastion scanned the vendor's items, coming to rest on one of the Stormwalker dolls.

"Ah, the young man has a keen eye," the vendor exclaimed. "Ever seen a Stormwalker?"

Bastion just shook his head.

"They're a scary bunch, they are," the vendor continued. "Nomads that kill us other tribes in weird ways. They live out in the Storm on purpose! 'Course, no one ever seen what they look like under all those rags and bandages. For all I know, you could be one!"

Bastion looked to Mira, concerned. But she just smirked and patted his shoulder.

"Don't worry, love," Mira said to Bastion. "No Stormwalkers here."

"But a few too many Eagles, yeah?" the vendor suddenly asked, his voice lowered to almost a whisper.

Mira paused, then nodded. "So you can help, then? Soon?"

Bastion watched them, confused. What were they talking about?

"Tonight," the man replied. "You two and three others. That's all I can afford to take. But you'll be outta here, safe and sound."

"Wait, what?" Bastion had heard enough. "What's going on here? What are you planning?"

The vendor glared at Bastion. "Is he not on board? You said he'd be ready."

"Ready? Mira, you're scaring me. This sounds like-"

"Things have gone too far," Mira reasoned with Bastion. "Please, love. Trust me."

"You're talking about treason," Bastion stated. "Jorus-"

"Shhh," the vendor warned as two robed Eagles strolled past them. Mira pretended to go over merchandise while the vendor monitored the Eagles until they'd left. Bastion seemed oblivious to all of it.

"The Eagles are heading for ruin," Mira claimed. "We can't stay here. As long at Jorus is alive-"

"Please stop talking," Bastion begged. "I don't want to hear this."

"You said he'd be ready, Mira," the vendor demanded. "I can't risk it if he ain't."

"He'll be ready," she replied. "Please, get us to the Pathfinders."

"The Pathfinders?" Bastion asked. "What do they have to do with this?"

"They need to be warned. We're the ones to do it."

"Be at the meeting place after sunset," the vendor said, eyeing Bastion warily. "This time tomorrow, you two will be Pathfinders. I promise."

"What?" Bastion exclaimed.

"We'll be married, in freedom," Mira said. "Thank you."

The vendor grinned. "It's what I do."

Mira turned from the vendor, and Bastion stared in shock. Then he caught up to her. "What are you thinking? This is illegal! If you get caught-"

"If *we* get caught, right? And we won't."

Bastion stared at her for some time. As he looked in her eyes, he saw fear. She really was afraid of Jorus, of what he stood for. But how could that be? Jorus was the word of all in the Eagle tribe. Jorus commanded respect. Or could that respect really be fear in disguise? What did his wife-to-be know that he did not?

"Last time, Bastion," she said. "Are you with me?"

Bastion thought of their future. Under Jorus's tutelage, they'd never go hungry. They'd be protected. They wouldn't need to worry about a thing. Yet Mira *was* worried. The love of his life felt something was wrong. Something about Jorus, about the Eagles, was not right.

Bastion sighed, whispering to no-one in particular, "I hope this is the right thing," then, to Mira, "I trust you. I'm with you."

Mira did not hold back tears that formed. "Thank you, my love. You'll see. And then we'll be free."

They left hand-in-hand.

After they were out of sight, the vendor leaned back against the rear canvas wall of the booth. He took notice of the shadow which loomed there, which had been there through the entire interaction with the young couple but hadn't moved an inch. They had not known they were being watched.

"It's done," the vendor mumbled. "They think they'll meet me at sunset, so I imagine they'll be in their tents until then."

The shadow said nothing.

"Easy target then," the vendor continued. "Look, I can't do this anymore. Let this be the last one, okay?"

Still, silence.

"At least be kind about it. The boy didn't seem to know."

But the shadow had gone.

In her tent, Mira had changed into lighter clothing for travel, with other gear stacked on her bed. The sun began its descent, so they would leave soon.

She sat at her small desk and looked in the cracked mirror by lantern light as she brushed her hair. The flower Bastion had given her rested in a glass with water on the desk. She again hummed a tune which she did not quite remember, but it made her happy, anyway.

She suspected Bastion was packing in his own tent. She felt bad. She'd sprung this on him in a matter of moments. She knew he'd invested so much effort into the apprenticeship. She knew it meant a lot to him. But Bastion meant the world to her. She couldn't lose him into the clutches of the dictator she had learned Jorus to be. Soon, they'd be free of the Eagles, and then they could build the life for themselves they deserved.

Mira placed her brush on the desk, and as she glanced back in the mirror, her humming halted. For just an instant it had seemed as if the gloom of the tent's interior had moved. She blinked and then saw it directly behind her. She stood to face the shadow that had intruded upon her.

"What is the meaning of-" Mira said, but winced when a quick blur of movement flashed toward her. She looked down to see a gloved hand retreating from her, and the handle of a knife protruded from her stomach. She looked back up to her unknown assailant, his identity hidden beneath a dark hood.

Mira turned from the stranger, approaching the desk. "Bast... Bast..."

Mira collapsed onto the desk, shattering the mirror and sending the lantern crashing onto the floor. The lantern's fuel instantly ignited and crawled its way along the nearest wall of the tent.

Mira spotted the flower, thrown to the ground and covered in the shattered glass. She tried to clasp for it. "Bast..."

She never reached it.

Unknown to either, Bastion made his way through the camp toward Mira's tent. In only the last couple of hours, Bastion's life had completely changed. One minute he was a loyal Eagle with aspirations to serve Jorus with honor. The next minute he'd become a blasphemer, willing to go against the word of Jorus and Eagles law. He'd sat in his tent, barely packing, rethinking what'd been said with the vendor. He'd gone over and over it in his mind, coming to the same conclusion every time; while he didn't completely understand Mira's motives, he was with her.

To the end.

He'd decided to tell her for certainty and made his way quickly to her tent. He was only a couple tents away when he noticed the orange glow from within. He raced to the tent, whipping the front open and ducking inside.

Mira was on the floor, blood pooled around her. The shadow stooped over her body. Bastion's entrance alerted the attacker, and when Bastion charged the figure, bellowing his rage, the shadow was ready. Bastion swung, but the shadow dodged and tripped the young Eagle, sending him sprawling onto the floor. Bastion instantly looked up at the stranger and stared wide-eyed as his attacker removed his hood. The look was unmistakable; face covered in bandages, eyes hidden behind tinted goggles. Mira's murderer was a Stormwalker.

Before Bastion could get to his feet, the Stormwalker was

gone. The young man could hear voices outside, nearby Eagles making their way to help.

"Help us!" Bastion cried.

He raced to Mira's side and turned her over. But Mira drew no life anymore.

"No," Bastion whimpered. He cradled his love in his arms, despite the growing fire around them. "No, no, no, no..."

He noticed her hand was outstretched toward the fallen flower. Gritting back his tears, and despite the inferno that threatened to consume them, Bastion took care to grab the flower and tuck in his belt. He then hoisted his love into his arms, only to find the fire upon them.

The lantern's fuel had caked everywhere, including the floor where Bastion had kneeled. The fire latched onto his left leg and crawled its way up his body. But he would not let Mira go.

Bastion screamed.

Outside the tent, Eagles worked feverishly to pour buckets of water on the tent. They heard the screams from within, but then stared in awe as the noise of pain joined with the image of Bastion, scarred and burning and screaming for his life and the life of his lost love. Bastion lurched from the flames, and despite the excruciating pain, carried Mira's limp body with care.

Then he stood, the two of them alight with the flames of agony, and roared into the night sky.

He should have died. He was sure of it.

Bastion spent weeks recuperating. The pain had been

unbearable, but the Eagles were known for having the most capable doctors available in the Eye. He survived.

But not without cost. His entire left side had changed forever, the scars a reminder of what he'd lost that night. He was fine with it. It was a grim reminder, a dark reflection of the side of him that had once held great love for a certain young woman. Only pain remained.

He should have died. Why hadn't he died?

Jorus had visited him. Jorus had revealed he'd chosen his apprentice, and that apprentice was to be Bastion. Despite everything, Bastion would still have the honor.

It wasn't until his final day in the bed that Bastion noticed the flower, long since withered and dried, curled on the counter.

Bastion finally cried.

Once he'd healed, Bastion made his way to the gravesite. He found Jorus waiting, alone, by Mira's grave.

Bastion noticed the headstone, a polished granite slab with the words MIRA - LOVED AND LOST. NOT FORGOTTEN carved neatly on the surface.

"I covered the cost of the headstone," Jorus said. "Least I could do."

"It was a Stormwalker," Bastion muttered, staring at the grave. Then, through a lot of still-remaining pain, he placed the dead flower on her headstone. "I know what I saw."

Jorus studied the young man. "I don't doubt you. As my new apprentice, you will find yourself privy to information not meant for the common Eagle, or any other tribe. That includes information on Stormwalkers."

Bastion eyes darted to the elder Eagle. "You know about them?"

"Among many other things. Come, it's time you learned how the world truly is."

Jorus turned and headed back for the Eagle camp. Bastion continued to stare at Mira's grave for some time, before relenting and following the older Eagle. He would become Jorus's apprentice and learn more about the Eye than he ever thought true. Then he would have his vengeance on the Stormwalkers, in true Eagle fashion.

Bastion never once returned to her grave.

CHAPTER 19

Bastion stood stoically at the ruins' entrance. The group just stared. His two guards were on edge, but Bastion himself seemed pleased.

"The hell you doing here, Bastion?" Aiden demanded.

"I could say the same," Bastion replied. "Without Daddy around, you really think you can succeed with this?"

"Hey!" Hobbes declared and marched forward, but Aiden stopped him.

"We have a mission," Aiden said. "And why did your master send you here? Eagles help no one but themselves."

Bastion shook his head. "Of *course* you blame your betters for your misguidance. No, instead I bring honest sympathies."

"I don't need your sympathy."

"Well, Lord Jorus sends his condolences none-the-less."

Hobbes laughed. "Somehow I doubt that."

"Actually," Bastion held his hands out as if in surrender, "I am here to help."

There was a long moment of silence while everyone tried to register what Bastion had said. Bastion? An Eagle? Help?

"Wait a minute," Sparrow spoke up, "Your people are against the entire reason we're out here!"

"Yeah," Larina agreed. "We're risking our lives so we can find a way through the Storm. We're doing this to help everyone. Don't tell me the Eagles, and especially Jorus, have had a change of heart."

"Don't confuse our decision to help as a union of beliefs," Bastion stated. "When we reach the end, and your heretical ideas are proven once and for all how false this all is, maybe you will finally see reasoning. Maybe then you'll join us under the law of the Eye, under Jorus. Be thankful we help you at all."

"You sound just like him. Jorus," Aiden muttered.

"I've learned from the best," Bastion replied. "But understand this. If you don't let me join, I will follow. And I will not be so... agreeable."

Finally Onyx emerged from his hiding place and approached Bastion. The Stormwalker's sudden appearance startled bastion as he realized who, or what, he was looking at.

"The Stormwalker," Bastion grimaced through gnashed teeth. "I should strike you down right here, you blasphemous poison!"

Onyx stared Bastion down through his black goggles. "I have no tolerance for your kind. Stay out of my way and leave your agendas to yourself. Understand?"

Bastion fumed, but upon realizing all eyes were on him, he soon regained his control. "Very well, Stormwalker. Blow your smoke. You'll soon find you are the one burning, not I."

The group rested in an uneasy sleep. Finch, wound up from the day's events and knowing he wouldn't sleep anyway, continued his watch at the entrance. Accompanied only by the glow of his lantern, he watched the Storm Wall beyond, and enjoyed the silence.

The strange sound of something skittering along the floor soon broke that silence, a sound that grew closer to him.

His fear eased, however, as a small spider-like creature emerged into the glow of his light. It moved on eight legs, but sported large pincers for hands. Pointed spikes protruded from every inch of its carapace, its tail equipped with dual barbs that dripped with venom.

"Hello there, pretty," Finch whispered in awe. He reached into his bag and pulled out a notepad, then made notes and sketches. He watched as it slowed upon reaching him, as if it studied him in return. This was definitely a welcome discovery, a new find to catalog in his studies back home.

He continued to make notes as the spider-creature skittered about, not seeming to dare to come too close to Finch. It kept stopping more than a foot from him.

Finch smiled and glanced back down to his sketch.

The spider-creature struck. The moment Finch lowered his gaze, it used its eight legs to launch itself into the air. It landed on his lap and instantly struck its barbed tail into his thigh, pumping its own brand of venom into him.

Finch yelped and dropped his notepad, then struck down with his hand to squish the thing. The spider-creature died instantly, but not before its many pointed and protruding barbs sank into his hand, delivering even more doses of venom.

Finch already felt the fire-like burn growing within, and he grabbed at his jacket sleeve, tearing it free. It horrified him to see the black venom coursing through his arm veins. They created a black web that pointed in all directions as they climbed toward his heart. Wide-eyed, Finch stumbled forward and tried to call for help. His throat had already swollen up, and no sound escaped. Acidic foam bubbled out his mouth while he gargled his final sounds.

The silence still flowed. Everyone remained in their slumber.

Then, with an ugly and awkward finality, Finch slumped to the ground, dead.

"Poor bastard," Vic said as he used a stick to poke at the remains of the spider-creature.

"Yeah," Creed nodded. "I seen what those things can do to the body. At least it was quick."

Larina shook her head. "We haven't even reached the inner Storm yet and we're already being cut down by it."

"What's done is done," Onyx continued the group conversation. "We must continue or his death will mean nothing."

Robin and Sparrow recoiled coldly at the statement, and Aiden could tell they were ready to speak their minds. But he knew they didn't have the time. "No, he's right. Anyone we lose fuels our reason to continue."

The group moved beyond the ruins of the Stone Man, directed for what was commonly known as the Wet Zone. Desert soon gave way to thickening grass, then the dry wind became a mist.

Onyx regarded the land ahead. "This is the right way. We will continue until midday."

"That's good," Aiden said. "Keep us going, Stormwalker."

"Hungry," Nemo stated.

"We must ration our food," Onyx said. "We have so little."

Aiden shook his head. "The lady says she's hungry. She eats."

Though his reaction was impossible to read, he faltered in his steps. "Fine. But we ration what we have." He then drew away from the group and up a hill. Then he disappeared from sight.

"What was that about?" Hobbes asked.

Aiden shrugged.

"So, how are the reading classes going? She gonna tell us more soon?" Hobbes asked.

Aiden beamed at Nemo. "She learns fast. She'll guide us once we're in lands familiar to her, remember."

Hobbes glanced to Nemo. "Uh-huh. What's your name, lady?"

Nemo just blinked. "Nemo."

Hobbes sighed.

"Give her time," Aiden said.

But before Hobbes could say any more, Onyx returned. He carried what appeared to be a cross between a walnut and a fern plant, but the size of a grapefruit.

"The Storm is dangerous, but it also provides," Onyx said as he snapped the thing in half, revealing an internal cavity filled with the inner 'meat' of the plant. He handed the halves to Nemo and Aiden. "If you know where to look."

Aiden examined the plant, then regarded the Stormwalker. "This is the same shell woven into your armor."

"That's right," Onyx replied. "What better protection from the Storm, than in the skin of those that bear it?"

Onyx continued on. Once he was out of earshot, Aiden turned to the others. "I'm getting how they survive out here."

"I still don't know about this guy," Hobbes said.

"Don't worry about him," Aiden reasoned. "If it comes to it, I'll deal with him. Okay?"

Hobbes sighed. "Okay. I guess so."

"Just follow me with this. Things are gonna work out."

Aiden and Nemo, who had been eating from the plant, carried on. Hobbes hung back a little, looking lost. He looked at his empty hands, then squinted and sighed to no one. "Maybe *I* wanted a nut."

CHAPTER 20

Four members of the Bird Tribe entered Jorus's throne tent. They gathered around Jorus's throne and instantly realized Jorus himself was not present. They also noticed the Eagle guards that lined the room.

Hawk was the leader of the group, and leader of the Bird Tribe itself. Muscular and commanding, he carried an axe looped in his belt.

Two aids accompanied him, plus his wife, Canary. She was much smaller than her husband, wiry but athletic, her darker complexion tried to hide an almost timid nature. She carried a rolled-up scroll with her.

"No more arguing, Canary," Hawk said. "I mean it. This could be our best chance."

"I still don't understand any of this," Canary countered. "Doesn't this feel off to you? Why suddenly now? We've tried for years to have straight talks with the Eagles-"

"I said no more arguing," Hawk declared. "We can't waste any chance we may have to strengthen a relationship, any relationship, with them."

"What relationship?" Canary asked. "The only times we see or hear of them, they're trying to kill us or convert us!"

"They're fanatics, yeah. It's what they believe. But they're still a strong force to be reckoned-"

"Which every tribe has paid for dearly to fight back against! Jorus is a dictator!"

"I agree with you," Hawk confirmed. "He's mad with his own power, and the Eagles don't see it. Or they're just too afraid to admit it. But a madman as our ally is better than a madman as our enemy."

"We should not be doing this."

"Why must you fight me so?"

"Because I married you," Canary stated, then lowered her voice. "You might be used to others taking orders, but I am your wife. I get to call you on your mistakes. Comes with the job, mister."

Hawk managed a grin. "You are trouble, lady. But really, appeasing Jorus, even if just to humor him today, could really help us."

"I just don't think I can agree with that."

"Still," Hawk regarded the other two Birds present for protection, "keep an eye out, yeah?"

Just then, the entrance curtains parted and the Eagle guards lining the room stood to attention. Jorus entered, followed by even more guards.

"Ah, Hawk," Jorus greeted. "I'd wondered if you'd travel here yourself. And the missus, too. Hello, Canary,"

Canary nodded and tried to hide her disdain. "Jorus."

"You called on us," Hawk said, "so here we are."

Jorus nodded. "My messenger's offer intrigues you?"

Canary stepped forward and presented the scroll, unrolling it.

Hawk replied, "We are open to a truce offer, but we have concerns."

"Oh?"

"Well, why now?"

"What do you mean?"

"Our whole lives, we have struggled to survive against the other tribes," Hawk explained. "If not in direct conflict, then in competition over raids and claims that are found. Year after year, we've reached out for friendship, with varying degrees with the other tribes. But not from you. Never from you. Again and again we've failed to gain an audience with the great leader of the Eagles. Until now. Now you've brought us here, with your own offer of truce. So I ask again, why now?"

"Very well," Jorus finally offered, not losing an inch of ground to Hawk. "It's this 'quest' that is unfolding, as we speak, to find some fanciful safe land beyond the Storm. I know you know. There were Birds at the tribal meeting. I believe there are Birds involved with the doomed group itself, yes? I'm concerned."

"Concerned for their lives?" Canary asked. "Or concerned they might make it, that they might be right?"

"They are not right!" Jorus lost his edge, the sudden fury flaring in his eyes.

Hawk reached for his axe and, seeing her husband's actions, Canary backed toward their guards.

But as quick as it'd appeared, Jorus's rage vanished again. "I am concerned for their souls. They are about to throw their lives away for nothing. They will never return, and those remaining in the Eye may continue to believe they'd made it to some fairy tale land. They may continue to believe in them."

"So, what you're really saying, is you are afraid of losing your sheep to other flocks?"

"Hand me the scroll to sign," Jorus said, and as Canary approached with the scroll unrolled, he took a quill in hand. "The catch is this. With this truce, two tribes become one. The Birds cease to be, and the Eagles grow. Then we begin work on bringing the other tribes into the fold."

Canary stepped back and looked to her husband with pleading eyes. But Hawk shook his head to console his wife's fears.

"Your messenger said nothing of that," Hawk said. "This is exactly what I was worried about."

"I need you to take that first step, Hawk," Jorus offered.

"Jorus..."

"Will you sign?"

Hawk looked to his wife again, and in her eyes he saw a great fear. All he saw in Jorus's eyes was hunger.

Hawk stepped back. "No."

Jorus faltered. "Say again?"

"No, Jorus," Hawk repeated. "Your 'one tribe' scheme will fail."

"You don't believe in peace in unity?"

"I do. But that's not what you're offering! I believe in my people and their hard work in this harsh world. It's a hard life, but it's their life. What you want, that's enslavement. We will not give up our freedom for your 'security'. No deal."

Jorus stared at them for some time, the slightest twinge appearing in his eye. "I'm disappointed, Hawk. I thought you an intelligent man, that you knew what was best for your people."

"You will not intimidate me into servitude," Hawk said. "And neither for my people. The Birds bite back too, Jorus."

"Are you sure this is the path you wish to take?" Canary rolled the scroll back up. "What are you going to do? Declare war? The Eagles are big, but not that big. Even you're not that crazy."

"Get out," Jorus said, and turned away from them. "Take your failed choices with you."

The Birds left as Jorus continued to stand defiantly. It wasn't until they were gone that he finally let out a breath and slumped. He wandered to his bookshelf and admired the collection he had accumulated from throughout the Eye, tomes he imagined had been highly regarded in the Old World. His eyes scanned the spines of many books, passing titles such as GREAT BATTLES OF WW2, D-DAY, and others.

"No, I will not wage war on the Birds," Jorus muttered to his guards. They followed his every move and word. "Not yet. But I can make them regret their decision. They are not the only other tribe in the Eye."

He moved to his throne and sat, hands clasped as if in prayer, but his meaning betrayed by the fire igniting in his eyes. "Fear. We have our faith. They shall have their fear, a fear that will stop their hearts cold."

CHAPTER 21

The rain fell as bullets. The wind, a budding hurricane, tossed debris about like grains of sand. The group struggled to stay grounded within the chaotic forces that pressed upon them.

As they journeyed, they passed more relics of the Old World. They came upon a large spire that rested broken in half on the ground, having snapped from its base long ago. The two halves now rested, partially submerged in an overflowed lagoon.

Further along they passed the shattered shell of what was once a majestic building with domed ceilings and large columns. The exterior seemed to have once been white, but the life of the outer surface had long since withered.

It watched the group, the inhuman-shaped thing, from within the oval-shaped room of the massive house. A clawed hand scratched the side of the window frame, the creature anxious as it stalked its prey. Then it disappeared again, slipping into the depths of the once-proud site.

The group faced an ever-increasing wall of force that grew by the moment and slowed them.

"This is insane!" Hobbes shouted, barely audible over the roar of the winds. "How are we supposed to get through this?"

"We should turn back!" Bastion warned. "It's a sign, a warning we have gone too far!"

"No!" Aiden countered. "We keep going!"

Bastion watched Aiden a moment, slightly awestruck at the young man's resilience, however misguided. "Look!" he called when he spotted what looked like an entrance to a cave, but with a rusted sign lodged above it.

The letters stamped on it were still visible; UNDERGROUND PARKADE.

"Another hiding place?" Aiden asked the Stormwalker. "Again?"

"The Storm is like water," Onyx said. "It comes in waves. We cannot force it. We wait until the next calm."

Aiden nodded reluctantly. "Everyone inside! Now!"

The group piled into the underground parking lot, escaping the Storm's chaos outside. Once inside, they found the parkade to be very dark, almost pitch-black. Aside from the muffled fury of the Storm outside, all was quiet save for the faint drips of dank moisture in hidden corners. A few rusted and gutted cars littered the ancient cement structure. There were also many holes of varying sizes that littered the cracked floor, which seemed to lead down into total blackness below.

As everyone settled, Hobbes flicked on his flashlight and scanned the area. "Well, it's better than a tent."

Aiden and Nemo found a clear spot to remove their gear. It was then that Aiden noticed just how drenched they were from the maddening rain outside. "We better get dried off."

Nemo at once began to peel off her layers of soaked clothing. "Naked?"

Startled at her instant disrobing in public, Aiden turned away while still shielding her from the rest of the group. Because he'd faced away, she couldn't see the rosiness that filled his face.

As the rest of the group found their ways to settle for the night, Onyx stood apart from them and stared into the darkness.

"What is it?" Hobbes asked the Stormwalker. "Something wrong?"

Onyx was silent. Finally, Hobbes gave up and used his light to inspect the nearby shell of an old car.

Alone again, Onyx glanced in Aiden's direction. He saw that Aiden and Nemo had changed into new clothes and now settled together against a wall, laughing and joking. The group had made a small fire, and in the light glow, Onyx could see that Aiden seemed happy.

Even without the darkness that surrounded them, because of the bandages that hid his features, no one could discern the smile that formed on the Stormwalker's face.

CHAPTER 22

The smallest tribe in the Eye, the Thorns were barely more than a few carts and horses. But what little they had overflowed with lush, Earthly bounty. The Thorns avoided the pitfall of vehicle use and opted to travel solely by pack animal. They also chose, many years in the past, to absolve themselves of guns, and instead defended themselves through use of spear and bow.

The other choice made by the Thorns generations ago was the exclusion of men. Thorn tribe members were female only. Whenever a Thorn came of the age to have a child, they would journey to other tribes to find a mate. They would conceive, then return to the tribe, leaving her mate until he was next needed. This exclusive lifestyle had served them well.

The night was quiet. A few small fires lit the weary tribe women as they prepared to bed down. Some finished their dinners, some tended to their animals. Barb and Ivy were there, keeping close to a fire to fight off the coolness of night.

A far-off rumble drew Barb's attention. As she looked past the camp perimeter into the darkness beyond, she witnessed a light appear up on a nearby hillside. As more Thorns noticed where she was looking, more lights appeared, one after the other, until a circle of singular lights formed a circle around their entire camp. Then the revving of dozens of motors sounded.

Before the Thorns could truly grasp what was happening, a wave of chaos hit the camp as the Dogs rode in on their bikes. They fired their guns in every direction with wanton mayhem. Many Thorn women fell before they could even rise to their feet, and many more scattered only to get run down by the besieging Dogs. Only a few handfuls of Thorns reached their weapons or their horses. Those that were able fought back, but it quickly became futile.

Barb and Ivy dodged and avoided oncoming Dogs on bikes and fought off any attackers that attempted to engage them by hand. Soon they reached the horse stable to flee on their own horses, but realized they were still unarmed. Still, they hopped atop their steeds and rode. The Thorn elder, who wielded a spear, soon joined them. The older woman rode with a ferocity that ignored her age, and she spurred the few remaining Thorns onward with waves of her spear. The small group reached the camp perimeter, but the unmistakable roar of engines told them the Dogs were close behind.

"Go!" the elder ordered. "Tell the others what happened here!"

Barb and Ivy chanced backward glances and saw the Thorn elder had turned her horse around to charge the oncoming Dogs. Horse versus a steed of steel in a game of chicken, she focused and threw her spear. It connected with pinpoint precision in the Dog's face and threw his lifeless body free from his bike. Her horse veered and avoided the empty chopper as it careened into the dusty ground in a heap. She then continued on against a second Dog. However, before she reached her target, a shot rang out from elsewhere and her horse collapsed, throwing her forward. She hit the ground hard and instantly felt the crushing weight of her horse roll on top of her.

The Thorn elder struggled and gasped for breath, unable to escape as a Dog bike rolled up to her. She saw the dirty pair of boots approach, and looked up to see the grinning face of Ted, a cigar propped between his teeth. He finished reloading his shotgun and brought it to bear on her, his grin never changing.

The blast of the shotgun echoed out across the vastness of the surrounding wasteland, and Barb and Ivy raced into the night.

CHAPTER 23

As their gear dried alongside their makeshift fire, the group huddled on the floor, their hungry eyes on cans suspended above the fire that bubbled with food. No one talked.

"I can't take much more of this," Creed finally muttered to break the silence.

Vic dropped an emptied can on the ground and wiped his beard. "The gear is dry enough, now we're just wasting time."

"Use your ears," Bastion said. "Don't tell me you can't hear that tempest still above us."

"I guess Creed can't sit still," Robin chuckled.

Vic smirked slightly.

"What're you smiling about, Dog?" Creed demanded.

"Just ironic is all," Vic replied. "We spend our whole lives moving. You'd think staying in place would be a nice change. Guess not."

As the group talked, one of the Eagle guards that'd escorted Bastion walked the perimeter of the firelight.

Larina turned to Onyx. "What's it like, being a Stormwalker?"

The Eagle guard turned from the group and worked at his robe to empty his bladder.

"Dangerous," Onyx replied flatly.

"Well," Larina continued, "I like a bit of danger."

Hobbes didn't like the sound of that, not at all. He moved to interject.

Meanwhile, the Eagle guard was busy urinating in the distance when he was suddenly and violently pulled into the surrounding darkness.

Hobbes stepped toward Onyx and Larina, but then Vic spoke up, interrupting him. "What is it like for you? You know, living out here, in the Storm. How do you do it?"

"Yes," Bastion added, genuinely interested. "How deep into the Storm do you travel, Stormwalker?"

Onyx stared into the meager fire. "As deep as needed to stay out of your way."

"What, we smell or something?" Hobbes asked, trying to crack a joke in front of Larina.

Aiden regarded Onyx. "Why do your people avoid the other tribes? You're seen so little, you're almost a myth."

"It's hard enough for your tribes," Onyx answered, "without our further drain on resources."

"You're saying you live out there, for our benefit?" Sparrow asked.

"You'd otherwise have us?" Onyx replied.

Vic then noticed a small light floating and bobbing around off in the dark. "The hell is that?"

Everyone stared.

"Anyone back there?" Aiden called into the dark.

No answer. The group cautiously rose and approached the light.

"It's beautiful," Larina whispered.

"Something's wrong about it," Bastion said, and as if on cue, the remaining Eagle guard stood in front of him before the light.

"Nah," Vic said. "Just something reflecting the firelight."

They got closer.

"I don't know," Creed offered. "It looks like a firefly, but it's so calm."

Realization then dawned on Onyx. He reached for his rifle, but it was too late.

Suddenly, a large shape burst forth out of the shadows and sank its needle-like teeth into the second Eagle guard, pulling him away in a blur. But then a second, even bigger one showed itself in the firelight.

The creature resembled a cross between a deep-sea angler fish and an eel, only tens of times larger. It weaved through the air, causing its hundreds of long, pointed teeth to gleam in the firelight. Lidless eyes glared at them, and a luminous orb danced on the end of a long tendril that protruded from its forehead. The long, serpentine body of the beast trailed off into one of the larger holes in the concrete floor.

They'd been tricked into thinking the small orb was a tiny wonder, only to discover it was a part of something much larger, much darker, and much more primal.

The group scrambled backwards, and some of them then noticed the blood spray that spotted their clothes. Some drew their weapons while others ran and hid.

"What was that?" Hobbes cried.

"Back to the fire!" Onyx ordered.

The group did as Onyx said and formed a circle around the fire, their weapons ready. While most failed to notice the second small light bobbing its way through the darkness toward them, Larina finally spotted it.

"Shit! Look out!" Larina warned.

Everyone spun to face the other light, only to see more lights come to life within the dark, each appearing as if from nowhere. From deep in the bowels of the darkness, they swung and swayed in taunting attempts to coax their prey to join them.

"What are those things?" Aiden demanded.

"I dunno," Vic said, "but I don't like them."

He fired, and a blood-curdling screech followed the blast. A slimy, swishing sound then announced the retreat of one monster back into the shadowed depths.

Aiden aimed his pistol at a light, then saw another light next to it, then another. There were far too many of them for the group to handle. They were surrounded. He then realized Nemo wasn't beside him. A quick, panicked glance to the side showed him she stood back-to-back with Robin and Sparrow, so he sighed a slight relief.

And then he saw the new light bobbing just behind them.

"Nemo!" he called.

Nemo glanced his way just as the slithering mass of eel-creature reared itself up and lurched forward into the light. Its scales glinted orange in the light, its powerful mass sliding along the crumbling concrete. Though its back half disappeared into the darkness below, what had pulled itself above to face them was still gigantic to view. The glint of fangs shot past the girls, who all ducked just in time. The creature then reared itself around for a second strike. As it did so, the rest of the group, those not occupied with angler-eels of their own, took aim and fired. Many of the shots rang true, and they heard shredding flesh. But then the beast dove at the girls again, and though it did not strike them for a second time, it slammed into the ancient and crumbling floor with great force. The creature, along with Nemo, Robin and Sparrow, vanished from sight in a cloud of collapsing dust and rubble.

"No!" Aiden screamed and raced toward the area of the floor that had become a dark cave below. Hobbes and Onyx joined at his side while the rest of the group kept the creatures at bay with sporadic shots.

Nemo, Sparrow, and Robin had fallen into an ancient sewer tunnel. It was dark and dank and had a shallow but a strong current of water that rushed past them at hip level. As they struggled their way out of the debris of the fall, they searched the walls for any handholds to climb back up.

"Help!" Robin called as she tried to jump her way up, but found no leverage to grab.

Up above, Aiden heard Robin's cry but couldn't see into the murky depths. "Are you okay?"

"We're all right!" Robin replied. "Just get us out of here!"

"Stay put! We'll throw a rope!"

Behind them, the girls felt the shifting of water and heard the rapid movement of something large approaching, and fast.

"Aiden, hurry!" Nemo screamed.

Robin drew her handgun and fired down the tunnel at the oncoming beast. It did not falter.

Then a plume of water hit them, and all three got thrown to the tunnel's floor. All they could do was stare up at the exit above them.

Hobbes returned with rope and threw an end down to the girls. "Climb!"

Robin spotted the rope end and grabbed it. She much preferred the continued gunfire above to the monster below.

After Robin ascended, Nemo reached the rope and climbed. As soon as she was high enough, Sparrow also began to climb. A final glance back told her the eel-monster was almost upon them again.

Robin reached the ledge of the hole and found a hand waiting to take hold. She took it and got swiftly yanked up to face the goggled eyes of Onyx. She then returned to the fire, where Creed continued to cover them with shots into the dark. The bobbing lights remained at bay for the time being.

Nemo reached the ledge next, and Aiden was instantly there to help her up. Then they turned to hold the rope as Hobbes reached for Sparrow.

Sparrow hoisted herself mostly out of the hole when she suddenly lurched back. Hobbes reached and grabbed her hands in his own.

Time slowed then, as Sparrow looked into Hobbes's eyes, the last person she would ever see. Her silent eyes screamed out far more than her burning lungs ever could, and then she got dragged back down into the abyss.

Hobbes stared at the space for a moment, but was then dragged back to the fire by Aiden and Nemo. Everyone kept their backs to each other and guns at the ready.

After some time, Onyx lowered his rifle. "Hold your fire."

"But we're surrounded!" Larina said.

"Don't you see?" Onyx continued. "Stay at the fire. They aren't coming any closer to the flames. They're afraid of it."

"How do you know for sure?" Bastion asked. "They're monsters!"

"They are still animals," Onyx countered. "Treat them as such."

"We have to get out of here and back up to the surface!" Hobbes said.

"We can't," Larina countered. "Hear the Storm still raging out there? We can't go out in that."

The sounds of the Storm had gotten worse. They were trapped.

"Onyx is right," Aiden allowed as he lowered his gun. "They aren't coming any closer to the fire."

"These creatures we can fight," Onyx stated, "the Storm, we cannot. We stay."

Hours later, the fire had died down. Everyone huddled around it, feeling it as best they could, knowing the flames had been their salvation through the night.

Hobbes leaned toward Onyx. "You ever seen these things before? I mean, you've been this deep before, right?"

"The Storm forced many forms of life to change since the Old World," Onyx nodded, "animal life especially."

"But those aren't just animals," Robin said. "They're monsters."

"These demons of the Storm are our jailers," Bastion muttered.

"Don't start with that," Vic growled. "We're just hittin' some bad luck."

"Do you deny your own eyes?" Bastion asked. "The Storm will only allow the righteous to pass its trials."

"Last I checked," Vic replied, "those things ate your people too."

Bastion hesitated. "Then they were weak."

The noise of the Storm outside finally waned, and rising daylight forged its way into the recesses of the parkade. As it did, the surrounding creatures' lights receded from view. The predators that had stalked them all night retreated into the depths below to await their next night of hunting.

"Survival of the fittest!" Hobbes laughed as he watched the final creatures vanish back into the dark.

"Survival is for those most flexible to change," Onyx said.

"They changed, and they survived," Aiden said. He stood and strapped his gear back on, then holstered his gun. "We will too."

CHAPTER 24

After searching for some time, Isaiah finally found Jonah sitting idly atop a truck on the outskirts of the Pathfinder camp. The elder man stared off into the sky, oblivious to Isaiah's approach. Isaiah sighed and climbed up with him.

"I've been lookin' everywhere for you," Isaiah complained. He glanced around, noticing the lack of a ladder or footstool Jonah should have needed to climb. "How'd you get up here, old man?"

"Look at that sky," Jonah said instead of answering. "So full. So clear. We of the Eye have never known a cloudy sky above us."

"Sure, it's pretty all right," Isaiah replied. "So I find you staring off at clouds while your grandson is out in the Storm risking his life?"

Jonah did not look at Isaiah, instead opting to keep his gaze on the open sky above. "Sometimes I understand why the Eagles admire it so. Eye of God and all that. There was a time people had a hard try to see the sky in its real glory. Too much fake light around, you see."

"I wanted to talk about the trucks," Isaiah changed the subject. "Some of the fleet is on its last legs. We'll only have two other full-sizers left for runs if we don't trade with the Dogs for repairs soon."

"The Stormmakers ruined the sky with their greed, you know. The land got poisoned, and the sky fouled up. That's what did it."

"Jonah, I got no idea what you're talking about."

Jonah finally looked to Isaiah. The old man grinned. "Well, you better figure it out before too long, my boy."

Jonah looked back into the distance, and his grin dissolved. In the distance, two figures on horseback rapidly approached.

"Stand ready," Jonah ordered, and forced himself to stand.

Barb and Ivy entered the Pathfinder camp. As Jonah approached, Isaiah close behind, he noted how worn and ragged the two young women looked. Their horses were strained and withered, panting and ready to collapse.

Barb dismounted and almost fell to her knees, but Jonah was there, and he steadied her. She then realized who it was that was helping her, and she sighed in relief. "Thank the Eye! Jonah, you've no idea…"

"Catch your breath," Jonah said.

She did. Ivy dismounted, tears in her eyes as she struggled to speak.

"Now," Jonah assured them, "from the beginning."

The following morning, Isaiah quickly rose and headed for Jonah's tent. His worry was compounded when he entered and found Jonah up and moving, packing a duffel bag.

"You been up all night?" Isaiah asked. "Do I wanna know what you think you're doin'?"

"Normally, no," Jonah replied. "But in this case, most definitely."

"No more riddles, Jonah. Not today, please. It's been a long night."

Jonah tied his bag shut and approached the exit. "No, you're right. No more jokes, Isaiah. Not anymore. This is it."

"Well?" Isaiah wondered. "What's the plan?"

Jonah paused. His trademark warm smile had gone, replaced with a hollow visage that fully revealed the truth of the old man's age. The once-energetic man finally looked tired.

"Just one last play," Jonah finally answered. "I doubt it will work, but I must try. Old man to old man."

"Try what?"

"I must go now."

"Go where? I'll get a truck prepped."

"No, my friend. Not this time."

"I don't understand. What are we gonna do?"

"Just concern yourself with your new role now."

As realization finally reached him, Isaiah shook his head in defiance. "Oh, no. You better be kidding. I can't."

"No more jokes, remember?" Jonah attempted a smile, but it quickly faded again. "The tribe will still need a leader. You're more than ready, my friend."

"No, I don't see it."

"It's plain as your face before me. Though you knew how important the expedition was, your real concern, as it's always been, was for the tribe. The people who are here, now. You watch over them every day. Don't think I haven't noticed."

Jonah left the tent then, which forced Isaiah to follow.

"But Deacon's gone," Isaiah said. "Aiden's gone. How can you leave too?"

"Because I must try what many have tried and failed before. I will battle madness with reason. I have to try, Isaiah. Pray I succeed."

"Now you're sounding like an Eagle," Isaiah muttered.

Jonah got into a truck and started it. "Good. For what I'm about to try, I sure hope I sound like one."

They shared a final look, and then Jonah drove away. Isaiah watched the truck depart, and as it became smaller and smaller in the distant dust, he stifled a breakdown that threatened to emerge. Then even the truck's dust tail was gone. Isaiah truly felt alone.

"Goodbye, old friend."

CHAPTER 25

Geared up and ready for the long trek ahead, the group emerged from the underground parking lot that had claimed many of their own the night before. But to their surprise and awe, they found the world around them had changed.

The once-soaking wet land around them had become a blinding-white frozen tundra. The ruins and structures that littered the area were coated in layers of frost and snow, and the winds had turned into a biting-cold sleet storm.

They stood in the aftermath of what seemed like a new ice age.

"What in the world?" Hobbes gasped.

"What is all this?" Larina asked as she squinted from the sun's reflection off the frozen ground around them. "The world has gone white!"

Robin bent down and scooped a handful of snow and inspected it. "It's beautiful."

"Onyx," Aiden said, "this is snow, isn't it? I've read about it in books."

Onyx nodded.

"Snow!" Robin exclaimed as she dropped her snowball, "Yes, I've read about snow! The frozen rain. 'A winter wonderland.' I never thought I'd see it."

"We've reached the Frozen Zone," Onyx stated.

"Frozen Zone?" Hobbes asked.

"The Storm has rings, like inside a tree," Onyx answered. "The weather can change drastically with each zone we pass through."

"We pass through circles?" Bastion said. "Like our own circles of Hell."

"We best get moving," Aiden said. "I don't count on freezing here."

"It's stinging my face already," Hobbes grumbled.

"We head through the city ruins," Onyx advised and pointed the way. "The structures will cut down the winds."

The group headed out, all taking care as they trudged through the snow. All except Robin, who gleefully skipped through the white powder.

"Snow!" Robin laughed. "I love snow!"

"Snow," Robin muttered later. "I hate snow."

Like the rest of the group, Robin had resorted to slogging through the cold and damp drifts about their feet.

As they reached the downtown core of the city, the group witnessed the snow-littered streets lined with tall, crumbling office buildings. Abandoned cars sat in the streets so long they seemed melded with the ground, like white, frozen lumps that sporadically rose from the concrete.

They soon arrived at two ancient skyscrapers that had long ago collapsed at their foundations. They had fallen into one another and created a haphazard arch over the once-busy city street. Their bulk took up the breadth of the street way, and there was no way around. The snow that covered their outer surfaces gave them the appearance of snow-covered mountains, and the group might have mistaken them for such if it had not been for the doors at street level. Recognizing the doors as the only route around the wreckage, Onyx signaled everyone to enter the building's lobby. The group followed him out of the freezing cold.

What had once been a high-end department store revealed its displays and merchandise to them, long since destroyed by the invading forces of the Storm. But the group immediately scavenged what they could. Amidst a circular desk labeled CUSTOMER SERVICE, Larina got a fire going, and the group huddled around it.

"Gah, I can't feel my face!" Hobbes moaned.

"It's still there," Aiden said.

Larina suddenly slapped Hobbes across the cheek. The young man glared at her with mixed shock and pain.

"Feel that?" Larina asked.

While the others laughed, Bastion ignored them and looked over their surroundings. There were multiple levels to the old store, reaching higher and higher, eventually into darkness where the building must have cracked and toppled sideways. The faintest hints of sky peeked through up there amidst the wreckage.

Bastion stared up in awe. "Never in my dreams did I see myself in such a place as this."

"You must have some boring dreams," Creed scoffed.

"This is more like a nightmare," Vic said. "I never been this cold."

"I would not condemn my worst enemy to a place such as this," Bastion declared.

"I think that's the nicest thing this guy's said," Hobbes muttered.

"Onyx, how much of this are we in for?" Aiden asked the Stormwalker.

Onyx was stoic as always. "Days, maybe."

"Days?" Robin cried.

"What you mean, 'maybe'?" Vic demanded. "You're a damn Stormwalker, ain't ya?"

Onyx was silent.

Vic stood, his large form casting a shadow over them in the firelight. Though his frame was imposing, the Stormwalker was not swayed.

"I find myself agreeing with the Dog," Bastion said. "If we are to freeze out here, perhaps we can at least die with some answers?"

That got everyone arguing among themselves. Onyx watched them for sometime, finally getting fed up with it all. "The Storm is not what you believe it to be."

The group paused.

Onyx regarded Aiden. "It is not simply bad weather."

He looked to Bastion. "Not some divine prison meant to punish us."

To Vic. "Not a trial of one's ego."

He regarded them all, "It is alive. It breathes."

The blizzards howled outside.

"It consumes."

Thunder echoed in the distance.

"It grows and shifts every day. The Storm can stretch for miles one day, and then only a few feet the next. A force of nature, so big, cannot be read so easily. My people still do not know all its truths. But we respect it. We respect its power, for there is no challenging it."

Vic glared at the Stormwalker, but finally sat back down. "The tribes have tried to fight the Storm for generations. Are we so foolish?"

Onyx shook his covered face. "No more than I."

CHAPTER 26

Jorus looked up from his book and smiled as he saw his Eagle guards escort a wary Jonah before him.

"Jonah. Lovely to see you again," Jorus commented. "It's been too long since your last visit."

"I swore to never return when you started making your own people take Walks," Jonah muttered.

"Ah, that," Jorus closed his book.

"But we need to talk," Jonah admitted.

Jorus placed his book down and approached the Pathfinder elder. He stared at him for some time, until, "Walk with me."

Jonah had journeyed to confront the Eagle leader, but watched as Jorus turned and exited the tent. But he had to try, he had to. Jonah had no choice but to follow.

The two men strolled at a leisurely pace. Jorus had his hands clasped behind his back while he smiled and nodded as they passed other Eagles. Jonah was not impressed.

"Look around, Jonah," Jorus eventually spoke. "Do you see people fighting each other here? Demanding scraps from one another? No one worries about where their next meal comes from because they rely on me to provide. And I always do. I always follow through with my word. Why do the other tribes refuse a better way of life?"

"You see people content to live the way you deem fit," Jonah countered. "I see people who gave up their freedom for 'security'. Tell me, Jorus. How safe are they, really?"

"They are safe because they pray to the Storm for it," Jorus answered. "Faith in the Storm will never wane."

"So you will continue to make them believe the same Storm that claims the lives of good people every day will choose to spare your Eagles?"

"Believe in the Storm, Jonah."

"I believe in people. The strength of our people is what will get us through. The will and drive of people."

"My people are strong."

"Your people are scared," Jonah argued, "of you."

"I can be... stern," Jorus admitted. "But look what happens when a stern hand is not in place. The Dogs are an aimless waste. But we strive for more. Because we believe in the Storm, the Storm gives us that strength. Ever since the Stormmakers were judged and deemed unworthy, the Eye has been our prison, but it's also our protection. The world outside the Storm is gone, the air poison to our lungs. Yet we endure. We are chosen by the Storm, Jonah. We survive. Does that mean nothing to you?"

Jonah shook his head. "The Storm you praise so much is about to ruin us all, chosen or not."

They continued to pass Eagles as they walked, so Jorus lowered his voice. "What are you talking about?"

"We all have our roles to play," Jonah answered. "We are Pathfinders in name for a reason. We study the maps. We chart the course. We see the patterns. We know where the Eye is heading, and that heading is our destruction. You've seen the signs, I'm sure, but you ignore them. You sit on your throne, happy to be in charge, but we all drown the same way, my lord."

Jorus was taken aback. There had been rumors, but they'd never been confirmed. Never in the known history after the Old World had there been a record of the Eye traveling out over open ocean. Could the old fool be right?

"Your fear has allowed you to send your only grandson into the Storm," Jorus growled. "What have you now? A few stragglers hoping for an answer we both know aren't coming back."

As they walked, Jonah noticed the occasional Dog present in the camp. He saw more and more and soon realized that Dogs had integrated themselves into the Eagle camp.

"And you?" Jonah asked. "I see new faces in your flock."

"The Eagles accept all," Jorus deflected. "Unity is key, Jonah."

"Unity," Jonah nodded, "as long as it's your vision of unity."

"You have a real chance here, Pathfinder," Jorus declared. "Deacon is dead and Aiden and the others are not returning. The Storm has claimed them, admit it. But you lead the Pathfinders now. They will follow you if you lead them here. Once the Pathfinders become Eagles, they will be safe."

Jonah looked around the camp as they continued. People seemed safe enough, but he found some Eagles averted their eyes or walked the other way as they neared. There was fear in the Eagle camp, fear for the master of theirs he walked beside.

Jonah steadily looked ahead. "No."

Their walk brought them near the perimeter of the Eagle

camp. As Jorus came to a stop, Jonah noticed a Jeep that was running, waiting for them.

"I'm sorry to hear that," Jorus sighed. "I really am. Get in."

That was it, then. Jonah knew he had failed. He had tried, steadfast in ensuring the Pathfinders' freedom. But it was not enough. There was no reasoning to be had here.

An Eagle guard attempted to lift Jonah into the Jeep, but the old Pathfinder resisted, instead climbing in under his own strained power. Jorus climbed into the front passenger seat and looked back at Jonah.

Jorus was grinning.

They drove out of the camp.

The Jeep was parked some distance away as Jonah, Jorus, and a couple guards walked into the wasteland. Jonah could see the Storm Wall in the distance.

"I suppose you know what comes next," Jorus said.

"You *did* have me take a walk with you," Jonah replied as he stared ahead.

"I respect you, Jonah," Jorus continued. "I do. So I will let you know that your people will be safe."

"Because you will take them."

"Yes. Some will resist, I'm sure. But they will have better lives as Eagles. Trust me."

"Trust?" Jonah laughed. "No one will ever trust you, Lord Jorus. It's sad that you will die alone."

Jonah then walked forward.

"We all die alone, Jonah," Jorus called after him. "You just get to go first."

As Jonah walked further into the wasteland, the Storm increased. The roar of wind and the flurry of sand blocked out most of the world around him. With each step, the going got tougher. His footing was unbalanced and he couldn't see more than a few inches ahead. He winced as the sand blasted against him and small lacerations formed on his exposed skin.

Jorus remained further back, hands held high as he praised the Storm.

Even further back, amidst the group of Eagle spectators, Doctor Reeves watched. As the image of Jonah vanished into the swirling Storm, Reeves turned away in despair. He realized all focus was on the scene ahead, and so he used that chance to sneak away.

Jonah stumbled to his knees as the Storm ravaged over him. The cuts and gouges grew. Blood from his scalp and forehead pooled into his eyes. His blood-tainted vision could barely see the forms of his shredded hands before him.

But then he forced himself back to his feet. He swayed at first, then planted his feet and faced the Storm. Jonah stood defiant as the Storm consumed him.

Jorus, satisfied, returned to the Jeep. He dared a final look back, and again that grin appeared. Always that grin.

Alone in the assailing Storm, Jonah reached out for anything, knowing it was a fruitless effort. But then there was something. His hand brushed a fabric surface, and suddenly it was his hand being grasped. Through his blood-caked vision, he could barely make out the shape. His delirium overwhelmed him then, and the old man gave up. Jonah collapsed into the embrace of something. Something man-sized. Something wearing a cloak and goggles.

CHAPTER 27

Deep in the department store, while most of the group slept by the fire, Aiden walked among the ruins and read old magazines on racks and ads on the walls, lit only by his flashlight. He still heard the blizzards raging outside.

He eventually reached an elevator with its doors stuck half open. He peeked inside. A suspended elevator box hung just below the doorway, its cables hanging taught. Aiden aimed his flashlight upward and illuminated a vast shaft above him, along with an open doorway one floor up. He carefully stuck his boot through the door and rested it softly on the stuck box's floor. There were creaks as the cables shifted, and dust filtered down from overhead. Then, suddenly, Aiden got yanked back out of the elevator to be stared down upon by Onyx.

"These ruins don't like to be disturbed," the Stormwalker muttered.

"I was curious," Aiden explained. "Your people live in the Storm, you're used to all this stuff."

"Not all."

"Still, this is all new to us. Shouldn't we learn while we go? Not just at the end?"

"Be careful what you wish to learn. The Storm has turned wonders of the Old World into dangers of our present world. These buildings have slept in the elements for a long, long time. Best not give them a reason to wake up."

"But I saw a way up."

Onyx pointed to a sign on the wall next to the elevator depicting stairs and an arrow that pointed upward.

"The first path," Onyx said, "is not always the wisest."

A look of humility crept over Aiden. "Stairs. Right."

"Be careful," Onyx said as he returned to the sleeping group and Aiden headed up the stairwell.

Neither of them noticed Creed, who'd been feigning sleep and listening to their conversation. He watched Onyx sit at a desk, then looked to the stairwell, the glints of the small fire reflecting in his eyes. He pondered.

Meanwhile, Aiden had crept up the stairs, which led to a set of doors that were chained shut. He ran his gloved fingers over the chain, noting the frozen state of the metal. Then, in one great tug, he snapped the chain, evidently brittle from the ages of frigid air. He cautiously pushed the door open.

Electronics filled the room beyond; radios, televisions, DVD players, computers, and more. Aiden began playing with buttons and switches, but nothing happened. There seemed to be no power. Nothing connected. Except, he realized, for a monitor mounted on a far wall. Wires connected the monitor to a dust-coated battery pack. The batteries in the pack were long past their prime, but Aiden grinned in realization. He pried the old batteries out, letting them thump to the frosty floor. He then excitedly unscrewed the end of his flashlight and ejected the batteries contained within. It elated him to find that both devices used the same battery type. He quickly connected them in.

The monitor thrummed to life, and the screen hesitantly blinked on. At first, Aiden only saw static. But then images started flashing into existence, a pre-recorded presentation meant to loop without end.

News footage that depicted chaotic events materialized before Aiden's eager eyes. It showcased maps of fallout zones, along with moving illustrations of flying missiles. Then the maps expanded to global measures, and fallout zones washed across the world.

"We don't know... longer... stay on the air," a reporter appeared and spoke in garbled static. "We fear... radiation... degrading climate. We advise... seek your nearest fall... shelter immediately... survive... oncoming super storm..."

Aiden practically pressed his face against the monitor, mesmerized so much by the dancing images. Then the screen went black as the batteries drained of their remaining life, and Aiden became startled to find Nemo's reflection staring at him in the monitor's blank surface. Aiden turned to see her standing quietly at the doorway.

"You scared me," Aiden said. "Why aren't you with the others?"

"Níorbh fhéidir chodladh," she replied, reverting to her language. "Nár mhaith leat a fháil caillte agus reo."

"Do you have anything like this where you're from?" he asked her.

Nemo spotted a pair of headphones and placed them over her eyes like a visor.

"Guess not," Aiden conceded. "Look at this. I found a picture box that works. See?"

He fiddled with the controls, then with the batteries, but it was no good.

"Well, it worked before. Damn," Aiden explained. "There was a voice talking about the Storm. I think I know how it began."

Nemo just stared at him.

"War," he continued. "The Stormmakers fell to war. Then came the Storm. I think that's what happened."

"War," Nemo repeated.

Aiden nodded. "There were symbols like the ones on the clicker boxes. Or like the bunker where my mother... I think it's connected."

A satisfied look spread over Nemo's face. "Tá sé faoi am a thosaigh tú ag figuring seo amach, Aiden. Chaitheann tú an oiread sin ama a insint dá chéile go bhfuil tú mícheart, go bhfuil tú riamh stop a bhaint amach b'fhéidir go bhfuil tú ceart go leor."

Aiden just stared.

"I mean, you smart Aiden," she tried again. "Learn soon."

Aiden just shook his head and laughed. "I think you're smart too. Smarter than you let on."

Nemo smiled and kissed his cheek. She then turned and left, leaving Aiden standing there somewhat puzzled but satisfied.

The group scoured the store and collected everything of use they could.

"You make any more sense of what she says?" Hobbes asked Aiden as they scavenged together. "You spend a lot of time with her. Any clues to what's next?"

"Yeah, you sweet on the lost girl?" Vic added.

"It's complicated," Aiden replied. "Between the crash and not remembering, then learning our language, I don't wanna push her too hard. She'll get there."

"But we need answers now," Hobbes said.

"Just look at her," Aiden nodded to her, across the room and giggling about something with Robin. I'd cross a thousand Storms for her, he thought.

"Hello, Aiden," Hobbes cringed, noticing the distant look his friend had.

"Let's move!" Creed announced. "Blizzard's let up. Better get back on the road!"

The group packed and left, and soon all was quiet. But then the frozen steel elevator groaned again. A clawed hand reached into the elevator shaft toward the box cables. The fingers of the hand flexed for a moment, then slashed. The elevator box dropped an inch, and then a deafening snap echoed through the building.

Outside, the group made their way through the white stillness left over from the previous night's blizzard. As they walked, the snap echoed out of the building behind them and bounced off the surrounding buildings.

"What was that?" Creed asked.

Then another loud snap sounded.

"Not another monster!" Larina hoped.

A final echoing snap sounded, and the elevator dropped free, crashing its way down the shaft. The entire fragile building shook at the commotion. The group cowered as the entire city block quaked around them.

"The whole place is coming down!" Hobbes cried.

Onyx glanced forward. "Run!"

The fallen skyscraper crumbled, and scattered debris fell in their path. They scrambled to avoid the large pieces that crashed into the surrounding grounds.

As they ran, Aiden glanced upward to spot yet another threat. The layers of snow that'd been resting on the skyscraper's outer surface shifted and cascaded into the street below. Before Aiden had time to warn them, the avalanche overwhelmed the group, and they all vanished in a flash of white.

Atop the snow, Onyx trudged in search of survivors. The Stormwalker paused and looked down at the powder beneath his feet, then swiftly plunged his hand deep into the snow. His hand then drew back out, grasping the coughing form of Aiden.

"What?" Aiden gasped. "How did... Nemo?"

"She's fine," Onyx nodded to further down where Nemo struggled to pull Larina from the snow.

Aiden got to his feet and stared at what remained of the skyscraper, then rejoined the others, who worked at digging out Creed and Bastion. But then, realizing all was quiet again, he glanced around in growing horror.

"Hobbes?", Aiden called. "Hobbes!"

Robin, Vic and Hobbes were nowhere to be found.

Aiden tried to race back to the ruins of the skyscraper, the deep drifts of snow constantly slowing him. Then, collapsing in fatigue and frustration, he tried to shovel away the snow with just his hands, but it was useless.

"No!" Aiden cried. "We've come too far for this, Hobbes!"

Bastion watched, then sighed and approached. "Aiden, stop."

"They're still down there!"

"I know. I do. But we can't help them."

Aiden pushed Bastion away violently. "They're under here! What's wrong with you? Dig!"

"They're too far down. It's a lost cause."

"You're a lost cause!"

"Aiden, stop," Onyx firmly placed his hand on Aiden's shoulder. "We can't help them now."

Aiden broke down and sobbed into the pitiful snow pit he had dug. The others remained quiet. Eventually, Aiden rolled onto his back and looked up into the sky. His tears had frozen solid to his face.

Bastion lowered his head. "Pray they be in a better place."

CHAPTER 28

Isaiah stood at a map table, surrounded by other Pathfinders, Barb and Ivy, and Hawk and Canary. He studied one map in particular.

"It's good you came to us, Hawk," Isaiah said. "All the Eye is at risk now."

"Jorus wants to combine the tribes," Hawk nodded. "But he's doing it under the mask of peace. We'd be conforming to his vision. We'd be under his control. He'd dictate how we live."

"And who we should be," Canary added.

"We'd all be Eagles," Hawk continued. "We'd always answer to him."

Isaiah nodded. "This is what it's come to. The Thorns have fallen because they resisted. But we can still fight back if we stand together. He can't fight both our tribes at once. The cost would be too great."

"He can if he has backup," Hawk said. "Jorus controls the Dogs."

Canary nodded to the Thorn girls. "The Dogs slaughtered

your people, but it was under Jorus's orders. With the Dogs under his control, his force is just as large as ours together."

"So we must unite to stand a chance," Isaiah said. "A united Eye may be the one thing that keeps us going. But it cannot be his Eye."

"Even united, do we stand a chance against them?" Barb asked.

Isaiah returned his thoughts to the map before them. "It's a chance. Things look grim. I've been over the supplies again and again. We're getting low, dangerously low. The Eye is passing over lands long since picked over. Our scouts would'a found something new by now, but these charts are saying otherwise. This is it."

"There must be unclaimed land, somewhere," Ivy said, desperate. "With just a little time..."

Isaiah tapped his finger on the map where land and sea met. "No more time. We're almost at the coast. Then no more land, period. We cannot move to the open ocean, it's just not doable. The mission stands. We need a way out of the Storm. We put our faith in the others to find the way. In the meantime, we make a change. There's nothing left to find. Now we must take it."

"Like the Dogs and their raids," Barb gasped. "We just saw our tribe, everyone we know, burn to the ground. They're all dead! That's what a raid is!"

"Barb, stop," Ivy whispered.

"If we raid, we're no better than them," Barb continued. "You really want that?"

"I'm out of options," Isaiah replied.

"Well, think harder! Deacon would have found another way to-"

"I ain't Deacon!" Isaiah snapped. "I'm tryin'. Believe me, I am. But I ain't cut out for this."

"Where is Jonah anyway?" Hawk asked. "Shouldn't he be in on this?"

"Jonah left," Isaiah muttered.

"What do you mean left?"

"He went to reason with that madman..."

Hawk's eyes went wide. "No..."

"We need to stop him!" Canary cried.

"It's too late," a new voice said. Everyone turned to the entrance to see Doctor Reeves standing there. He held Jonah's cane.

"What are you doing here, Eagle?" Barb accused.

She marched to Reeves and grabbed him by the collar. She wound up to strike him, but Canary intervened.

"Hold it!" Canary said. "Let him speak."

Reeves backed away but held the cane outward. Isaiah took it.

"What did they do to him?" Isaiah asked.

"He fought," Reeves said. "Jonah fought for all of us. But Jorus is... insistent."

"You mean insane," Hawk muttered.

Isaiah glared at Reeves. "Where is Jonah?"

Reeves looked to the floor. "Jorus made Jonah take a Walk."

Silence.

Then Ivy finally spoke. "He was alone, all alone in the Storm? How could they do that to him?"

"It will only get worse," Hawk said. "Please, Isaiah, join with the Birds. This can't keep happening."

Barb nodded, gesturing to Ivy. "Count us in."

"I agree," Reeves said. "This madness must end."

Isaiah looked at the cane he held in his hands. The insignificant thing that had belonged to the man he cared so much for had hidden weight to it then. Damn you, Jonah. Was this what you had in mind for me? It was a choice between two dark fates. Fight Jorus and hope to hold on to their freedom, which would likely come at the cost of many lives, or give in and keep his people alive, but at the cost of their freedoms. Jonah, Deacon, Aiden, what would you have done?

He knew then, the answer all three lost friends would have given, what they would want for their tribe's future.

"All right. Yes," Isaiah agreed. He shook Hawk's hand. "The Pathfinders will fight with you."

"Do we have a plan?" Ivy asked.

Isaiah nodded to the doctor. "Have they yet mobilized against us?"

Reeves shook his head.

"Then we take the fight to them, before they are ready," Isaiah confirmed. *For you, Jonah.* He turned to Hawk. "Gather the Birds. The tribes are going to war."

CHAPTER 29

The subway tunnel was dark and dank. The rail lines that traveled the floor had flooded, but the sides of the tunnel still held dry ledges. At one end of the tunnel, the recently collapsed structure of the broken skyscraper had smashed through and left a slope of rubble and snow.

Suddenly a chunk of rubble shifted and fell away to reveal the dust-covered form of Vic, hacking and coughing at the dust in his lungs. He forced himself to his feet while he pressed his back and shoulders against the debris atop him. As he rose, the huddled bodies of Robin and Hobbes emerged. The three of them then crawled out, and Hobbes quickly used his flashlight to illuminate the tunnel they found themselves in.

Hobbes whistled as he noted the skyscraper's structure looming above them. "How'd we live through that?"

"Luck of the moron," Vic replied, "as my brother would say..."

"Not likely," Robin said. "The ground under us three collapsed first. I saw it. But where are the others? Did they make it through?"

Neither of them had an answer for her.

"Aiden!" she yelled. "Larina!"

Vic quickly silenced her with a hand over her mouth. "Quiet, girl. Forgotten about the things that lurk in these tunnels?"

Hobbes aimed his light over the surfaces of the water about their feet. "If those things are down here-"

"I'd rather not find out," Vic finished. "Let's get outta' here."

"But what about the others?" Robin asked again. "What If they're caught in all that wreckage up there?"

"Nothing we can do from down here," Vic said.

Hobbes shook his head. "They had to have gotten out. They had to."

"But how do you know?" Robin whimpered.

"Well, Onyx is with them, right?" Hobbes realized. "If they got that guy with them, then they're in good hands."

"But they've also got Bastion up there," Robin responded. "He's probably trying to force Aiden to end the mission right now."

Hobbes shook his head. "No. We've come too far to give up now. No way is Aiden gonna quit. When they can't find us, they'll continue as planned. Best we can do is catch up with them."

Vic groaned. "And we're supposed to find our way without the Stormwalker?"

"Oh. Right," Hobbes conceded as defeat overtook him. But then a realization dawned, and he grinned a wide grin. He then pulled his pack from his back and pulled out a tattered map. He laughed. "They might have a Stormwalker, but we have the charts."

The three of them peered at the paper, where many paths of the Storm had been traced again and again over the generations. Also illustrated on the map were the remains of once-great bridges that crossed over a large body of water. The bridges seemed to be the only way across, so it was the only choice. It would force Aiden and the others that way, he was sure.

It was then Vic's turn to smile. He slapped his large hand on Hobbes's shoulder. "Okay, Pathfinder. Time to live up to your namesake."

Then the clicker box in Hobbes' pack sounded.

"I did not wanna hear that down here," Vic muttered.

The clicking increased.

"They're coming!" Robin squealed.

"Up top!" Vic ordered. "Now!"

The three scrambled over debris to force their way back to the surface.

Aiden and the others made their way out of the snowy ruins of the formerly grand city. As they walked, Aiden paused every few minutes to look back at the path behind them.

Creed walked next to Bastion and noticed Aiden's continued pauses. "He keeps looking back to see if they're coming."

"Aiden holds on to hope," Bastion said. "Something most have lost these days."

"So much for the kid being a leader."

Bastion glanced to Creed. "His best friend followed his lead and died. That should give any leader pause."

Creed grimaced into the cold wind. "Gonna say a prayer for us, Eagle?"

"I'm afraid," Bastion replied as he looked up into the

swirling mass of winds above them, "that in this tempest, I would not be heard."

Soon the expedition put the city far behind them and exited into open wild. As signs of the long-forgotten metropolis gave way to sprawling fields and forests of nature, the group found themselves in awe of the untouched blankets of snow the world offered. That sense of awe continued as they reached the shore of a massive lake. The lake itself had frozen solid, a wide stretch of untouched ice and snow that reached long past their horizon. The remains of collapsed suspension bridges stood in the distance, their usefulness faded into history.

"It's all so still," Larina whispered.

Bastion pointed to the broken bridges. "Are those the bridges we mean to cross?"

"Doesn't look like they're gonna bridge anything anymore," Creed said.

"The charts, Pathfinder," Onyx said. But Aiden didn't notice as he stared off into the white distance. "Aiden."

Finally, Aiden gathered his wits and searched his pack for the map. Soon, though, he withdrew empty-handed and forlorn. "I... I don't have it."

"What?" Creed lost his composure. "You don't have the map?"

"Hobbes..." Aiden realized. "Hobbes had it..." He then slumped to his knees, despite Nemo and Larina trying to hold him up. "I lost them. I lost the charts. Everything's lost!"

Nemo tried to comfort him, but Onyx shooed her away. She backed away as the Stormwalker swiftly approached. He grabbed Aiden by his vest and hoisted him roughly to his feet.

"Listen to me, you sniveling little Eye-dweller," Onyx

growled. "Out here, the Storm doesn't revolve around you. Out here you revolve with it!"

The loud outburst from the normally stoic Stormwalker shocked everyone, but none more so than Aiden.

"I gave up everything to see you through this," Onyx continued. "I'm not letting you throw away our progress just because tragedy struck you a little closer than you'd have liked." He then let go of Aiden and let the young man regain his composure. "Loss is our lives. Loss is all our lives. But we have luck on this day. The Storm has provided us a bridge."

He indicated the vast frozen lake before them. He then took the lead and guided everyone out onto the ice, save for Aiden, who remained where he'd been manhandled by Onyx only moments before.

Nemo went to his side. "I sorry you're sad. I sad too. But must go now, yes?"

Aiden watched the others make their way over the ice, then sighed. He nodded, and together, he and Nemo set out onto the icy surface.

As they left the shore, they found the winds increased drastically over the open ice. Snow and flurries wrestled upon them and bit them to the bone.

After some time, Larina spotted something in the distance. Many small dots hopped up and down on the ice, outlined against the stark white of the surrounding blizzard. "Do you see that?"

The group paused. As Larina pulled her goggles off, she forced herself to squint against the oncoming winds and make out the shapes before them.

The dots were little birds, an owl almost as perfectly round as a ball, about six inches in diameter. Their feathers seemed solid, hardened into a protective shell similar to the nut plants found in the Storm.

"Onyx, what are they?" Larina asked. She approached the owls but Onyx stepped in the way to halt her.

"Stop," he warned. "It's not safe."

"Why? They're the first live game we've seen in a long time. They'd be easy to catch."

"If you think they're easy targets, then so do other creatures," Onyx replied. "Bigger creatures."

"More monsters," Bastion whispered.

"The only monsters I've seen live in the Eye," the Stormwalker said, then slowly scanned the horizon. "These are just animals living their lives. But don't get between a predator and its prey."

Further down shore, Hobbes, Robin and Vic made their cautious way onto the ice. As they walked, Robin's face lit up in a grin. Off to the side, a bunch of owl-balls huddled together. She hurried over to them and was ecstatic to find them not fleeing from her. They seemed completely out of it, even letting her take one in her hands. The owl-ball stared up at her with big, golden eyes and let out a light coo as she snuggled it.

"It's so cute!" she squealed. "I want all of them!"

"Trust a Bird to find a bunch of birds," Hobbes smirked.

"Bite size," Vic licked his lips. "I like them already."

"Don't you dare!" Robin cried. "These birds are not for eating!"

"Listen, girl," Vic said, "we got a few scraps of food

between us. We could roast these things and eat them on the move. Perfect."

"The big guy's got a point, Robin," Hobbes admitted.

Robin looked horrified. "These are the first nice things we've found on this forsaken mission. Can't you just let me enjoy this?"

Hobbes and Vic each took an owl in hand and noted the birds still did not move. They just stared up blankly with their big eyes.

"These things are covered in frost," Hobbes said. "How does something so small survive out here?"

"They don't even run away," Vic said.

"Well," Hobbes said, "we're probably the first people they've ever seen. Maybe they just don't know to fear us."

"Because you want to eat them?" Robin chastised.

"Well, yeah, there's that."

Then a loud crack echoed out in the distance. All three looked into the blizzard but saw nothing but white.

"The ice might break up," Vic said. "We'd better go."

The owl-balls then dispersed, hopping away from the three travelers.

Another crack occurred, only closer.

"They're probably spooked by the noise," Hobbes noticed. "Okay Robin, come on. We're all hungry."

"I know, I know," Robin sighed. "I just wanted to enjoy the moment."

And then an eight-foot-tall spiraled spike bore up through the ice from below and struck up between Robin and Vic, which made them scramble back. Then the spike drew back down below the ice and disappeared.

"What was that?" Vic yelled.

Another spike shot up just behind Hobbes. Then another. And another.

Hobbes and Vic moved to gather up Robin, who was still sprawled on the ice from the initial strike. But before they reached her, another large spike shot up and shifted the surrounding ice. Hobbes and Vic, along with several owl-balls, got tossed around the ice as a great, monstrous shape crashed its way to the surface.

It was a large species of narwhal. The size of a truck and vicious, the whale thrashed on the ice and scooped up owls into its large mouth. Then it slid back into the depths, leaving plenty of owl-balls remaining.

"Move!" Hobbes screamed.

They ran. Narwhal horns speared up around them as they moved across the icy surface, narrowly missing with each passing step. Behind them, many blubbery masses of whale smashed up onto the ice and feasted on the plentiful owls that scrambled in all directions.

As Robin moved, a horn suddenly pierced its way up and into her backpack. She got hoisted up with it and dangled in front of the great beast's gaping mouth.

Vic instantly sprung and pulled a hammer from his belt. He gripped it tightly and delivered a mighty swing upon the length of whale horn. He struck again and again, as the narwhal threatened to bound back into the icy depths and drag little Robin along with it. Finally, just as the narwhal slunk back to the water, the horn shattered and Robin fell into Vic's arms. They ran, and the beast conceded its defeat, and retreated to the ice waters below.

Once they were clear, Vic pulled the remaining shard of horn from Robin's backpack. He raised it high in the air and roared a bellowing victory cry that echoed out across the vastness of ice.

"Did you hear that?" Aiden asked Onyx. He could discern nothing out there in the icy fields.

But the Stormwalker knew. "Dinner is served."

As night descended, a small firelight illuminated a cave on the rocky edge of the frozen lake. Around the fire sat Vic, Hobbes, and Robin. The latter sported a horrified look as she watched small chunks of meat cook and sizzle in a couple metal pans over the flame.

Vic and Hobbes happily devoured the cooked meat while Robin rolled the narwhal horn in her hands. Between bites, Vic slid a pan of bird meat her way, and she glared at it in disgust.

"Not much else to choose from," Vic uttered through a mouthful.

"Unicorns *do* exist," Robin sighed.

"Yep," Hobbes agreed, "and they almost killed us."

Vic burped. "Good eatin'."

As Hobbes chewed away at his dinner, he looked over the chart again. He traced their hopeful trail ahead a few miles and stopped at a circled area with a building drawn in it. "I think this is the next likely place to find the others."

"If it's still there," Vic grumbled.

"It's the only structure for miles, and the others will need to rest first before going further."

"If they're even alive," Vic grumbled again.

Robin suddenly wolfed down her meat, surprising the others. "What? You said there wasn't much else."

The guys chuckled as she went to set out her bedroll. Then, almost instantly, she was sound asleep.

Hobbes leaned closer to Vic and then whispered, "She likes you, you know. If it wasn't for her, the others would'a thrown you back out into the Storm."

Vic let out a sigh. "Didn't think we'd make it far enough for me to start bein' liked. Figured I'd be dead by now."

"Why bother to join? I know your brother ditched you, but-"

"Because a good deed deserves another," Vic cut in. "I think I owe that girl a few good deeds."

"She saved your life."

"Yeah, but her brother..."

"Her brother?" Hobbes asked, and then realization dawned on him. He glanced at the sleeping girl, but seeing no signs of her being awake, he hissed through clenched teeth. "You killed Crow?"

"That was his name?" Vic bowed his head, keeping his eyes locked on the fire.

"And you're choosing now to say something?"

"I've protected Teddy from himself for a long time," Vic tried to explain. "If I hadn't acted in that bunker, then none of us would have survived."

"What about all the raids you Dogs go on? How many people have you killed?"

"How many have *you*?"

"Not the same."

"Isn't it?"

Robin shifted a little, alerting them. But she remained asleep.

"You gonna tell her?" Vic asked.

Hobbes shook his head. "You can do your own dirty work. If you think she should know, then tell her yourself."

With that, Hobbes went to his own bedroll. That left Vic alone at the fire, alone to ponder into the night.

Robin awoke to the smell of cooking meat that accompanied the dawn. She instantly saw Vic sitting at the fire as he stuffed remains of the previous night's dinner in his chomping mouth. He had meat and grease smeared in his beard.

"How do you eat like that?" Robin asked, a little repulsed.

"Dogs are survivors," Vic replied as he gulped down the mouthful. "You'd be surprised what passes for food in the Dog camp."

"I wouldn't be surprised," Hobbes muttered as he rose.

"I always finished my brother's scraps too," Vic continued. "How else you think I got so big?"

"My brother always said I was too picky," Robin said as she joined him at the fire. "He said I would have starved long ago if I'd been in any other tribe. That if I got any smaller, the chickens would eat me. So he cooked me fresh eggs whenever I complained."

Vic feigned a smile. "I'm sorry, Robin."

Robin looked confused.

Vic noticed the grim look Hobbes had, but he continued to fight for the words. He assembled them in his mind, but nothing seemed good enough. Then a spark went off, and he pulled something from his coat pocket. "I tried my best, but..."

In his hands he held Robin's unicorn figurine. It'd been scratched up and one of its front legs was gone, but it was unmistakably hers.

"I found it out there, before I met all you. When I was... on my own. The leg was broken when I found it," he said. "I wanted to carve a new one, but we've never been in a good place to-"

Robin interrupted him by suddenly hugging him tightly, her small frame dangling around his large neck like jewelry.

"I like him better this way," she whispered between warm tears. "Thank you."

Vic paused, but then found the nerve to hug her back, the man who was so foreign to affection.

CHAPTER 30

Isaiah stood atop the tanker truck in the Pathfinder camp, Hawk and Canary at his side. Barb, Ivy and Reeves were also present, intermingled with the Pathfinders and Birds that stood before Isaiah. The crowd stood as one.

"I know you'd rather see Deacon standing here," Isaiah spoke to the crowd, "or Jonah, or Aiden. But I'm what we got, and I plan on making use of that."

Hawk stepped forward. "We're asking a lot of you all. We know that. We're talking about risking our lives, all our lives."

Isaiah nodded. "We risk our lives every day in the Eye, but they are our lives to risk."

"Jorus means to change that," Hawk continued. "Do we really want him in control of our very lives?"

"Jorus promises peace, yes," Canary said. "But peace at the cost of freedom is not true peace."

"We can't let this continue," Isaiah said.

"We must fight!" Hawk roared.

The crowd reacted. Everyone was in agreement. They had set the kindling. All it needed was the spark.

Isaiah calmed, then asked, "Are you with us?"

The crowd erupted in the affirmative. Cheers and applause of support filled the area.

"Thank you," Isaiah replied, "all of you. We can't promise we'll win this fight. We can't even promise it's a fight we'll return from."

"But we can promise to resist," Hawk agreed. "We can promise to show Jorus he is wrong. He will never control us!"

Canary raised her fist in the air. "Live or die, we dream free!"

The crowd cheered again.

"Jorus has worked so hard to drive the tribes apart," Isaiah said, "but now I see he has failed. He has only driven us closer together!"

"Let's make sure Aiden and the others have a free home to return to," Hawk called. "Let them return to a free Eye!"

"For a better life!" Canary yelled.

"For Jonah!" Isaiah called.

"For the Thorns!" Barb shouted.

"For the mission!" Hawk added.

Isaiah nodded and lifted both his fists in the air. "On this day, we fight as one!"

Once more the crowd cheered.

It was time.

CHAPTER 31

Hours passed. Though the torrential weather raged around them, it paled compared to the floods of grief that echoed within Aiden.

Vic... Robin... Sparrow... Finch... and Hobbes.

Hobbes was gone. Hobbes was dead. His best friend was dead.

Nemo tried to comfort him. She would hold his hand. She would share her food. She would smile. But none of it worked.

Deep within, Aiden was lost.

A few feet ahead, Larina fought back her tears. She told herself it was to keep them from freezing to her face, but really it was pride. Her Thorn pride that made her go on this journey to prove herself. Her Thorn pride that made her feel stronger than others around her. Her damned Thorn pride that had kept her from letting Hobbes warm up to her. And now he was gone. That insufferable, annoying, loud-mouthed-and-surprisingly-charming guy was gone.

For once, even her Thorn pride couldn't tell Larina what to do next.

Further ahead, Bastion and Creed conversed with each other. Onyx continued his ever-silent vigilance a few meters ahead of them.

"What now?" Creed asked. He didn't really expect an answer. He knew the Eagle whelp wouldn't have one without his Master Jorus around to whisper orders to him. This whole mission had been a disaster. The list of losses was growing, but Creed praised himself not to be added to that list.

What now? Bastion pondered to himself. *What now indeed?*

"The Storm tests us," the young Eagle finally responded. "If we falter, the Storm deems us unfit. The Storm claims us. The Storm consumes us."

"The Storm this, the Storm that," Creed scoffed. "Nah, boy. We're still here 'cause of luck. That's it. We could go at any moment. That's the facts."

"Your lack of faith in the Storm won't change anything, Creed. It judges you whether or not you accept it."

Aiden paid no mind to the interaction ahead. His thoughts were many miles away, back under an avalanche of debris and snow...

"Aiden," Nemo spoke quietly. "Not the end. We go, for future, right? For life?"

Her voice pulled him back for a moment. "Yeah. I guess so."

"Then we honor their memory. No give up. Make life count."

"Count for what? They're gone."

"Yes, gone. But you here. We here. Remember them. Do it for them."

He looked to her then, and found that steely resolve he'd first seen the morning of the initial tribal meeting, the morning Onyx had emerged and changed all their lives.

No, that wasn't when everything changed, Aiden realized. *It was the plane. It was Nemo...*

Aiden sighed and managed a nod. "You're right. We keep going. We see this through, for them."

Nemo nodded, but then they paused as the group realized Onyx had stopped. He stood still, his head turned one way, monitoring something in the distance.

"What?" Creed asked. "What you hear, Stormwalker?"

Onyx didn't reply. He just stared out in the distance. Then, finally, "It's out there."

"We hear nothing," Aiden said.

"Nothing over the wails of the Storm," Bastion agreed. "What's out there?"

"Not another monster, please," Larina whispered.

"Don't you see?" Bastion pleaded. "It stops us at every turn! We are not meant to get through the Storm! Everything out here can stop us or kill us! We have no hope!"

"Shut up, Bastion!" Creed roared. His panic showed itself, and he didn't appreciate being treated in such a manner. He pulled his kukri blade from his belt. "Shut your mouth before my blade does it for you!"

"Quiet, all of you!" Onyx commanded. He then turned off their path and walked in a seemingly random direction. "They are this way."

As the Stormwalker continued, the rest of the group

lingered. They regarded each other before each turned to Aiden.

"Your call, Aiden," Larina said.

Aiden watched Onyx fade into the blizzard, then nodded.

Okay, Hobbes. Some adventure, right?

"Let's go."

The trek through the snow was uneventful, the only constant being Onyx in his single-mindedness.

The group followed, though with palpable hesitation. Their doubt was rising, Aiden could see. Soon all that would remain would be hopelessness.

Onyx stopped. The group mimicked him, but Aiden had had enough. He stepped forward to confront the Stormwalker.

Then he heard the sound too. A voice.

Speech, too faint to understand, danced on the wind. The falling snow muffled the sound. It was definitely there.

A voice called to them.

The group moved as one, suddenly spurred onward by the new element. As they made their way, the volume of the speech grew ever so slightly.

"We... here... exist... are... Soon... Find... exist... Help... message..."

Finally, Aiden found he could make out words. "I hear it!"

The others agreed as they, too, discerned the strange speech. Onyx raised his rifle in the air and pointed it westward. "This way!"

The group approached the foot of a hill, and as they ascended, the voice became slightly more clear.

"We are... exist... were... Soon few... us... exist... Help... us... This..."

They crested the top of the hill and a strange structure came into view. It had a similar shape to the bunkers and military sites they were used to seeing in the Eye, but this building had one glaring difference. Atop the roof sat a large circular dish. Its surface had broken and lost much of its plating, but the shape remained. A large antenna rose from the center of the dish.

The voice came from within.

"We... We... were... Soon... We... us... repeats..."

The group regarded Aiden. He stood at the door and soon forced himself to push on the bar. The door, having not properly moved in generations, fought back. But a second, more forceful push and the door gave way, and creaked inward to expose the room ahead.

Desks, covered in ancient dust, lined the walls and created rows in the middle of the room. Long-dead computers sat atop the desks, faceless and empty of life. The group soon realized the voice did not originate in the room. Another door stood directly across from them.

The group passed the computers, unaware of the powerful machines they once were. Still, the voice spoke.

"We are... We... many... Soon... We... Help us... This message..."

Each person carefully strode through the next doorway, their guns and blades at the ready. The voice continued.

"We... Help... repeats..."

But no one was there to greet them. The room was empty, save for a single terminal in the middle of the room.

The desk was a much larger and more detailed piece of furniture. Wooden and intricately carved, it depicted designs unknown to them, etched into the sides and top surface. Like the desks in the previous room, this desk also had a computer sitting atop it.

But this computer had power.

The screen was active. The computer's desktop showed the image of a child and a dog running through a field, and the picture was partially obscured by the one program window that ran. It was an audio track, and as it played, the program's cursor traveled along with the sound bar.

"We... here... We were... Soon... exist... This message..."

The sound was loud this close. The group watched as the audio track reached its end, only to then refresh back at the beginning. The program was on a loop.

"What is this?" Creed asked.

Aiden looked to Onyx. "You knew this was here?"

"No, but I've heard stories," Onyx replied. "Something we don't understand."

"Something the great and wise Stormwalkers don't have an answer for?" Bastion muttered.

Onyx was unfazed. "There are mysteries in the Storm more vast than any realize. This message, which has played for years, is such a mystery."

Bastion then noticed a small blip that occurred each time the audio track reached its end and refreshed. Every time the cursor reached the end of the track, the program seemed to pause just for a moment. Bastion waited for the track to finish its next play through, then on a complete guess, he swiped his finger on the cursor just before it began again.

Everyone jumped back as a second window opened on the desktop. It contained the audio track, but also included a video image.

The group stared at the footage of a person cloaked in

shadow. The person was bald, but the darkness kept any other features from being seen. They couldn't even tell the person's gender, as the voice was scrambled, mimicking the monotone essence of a computer.

"We are here. We exist. We were many, soon few. Find us. Help us. This message repeats."

The voice spoke as the shadowed figure remained still. The room surrounding the figure was the same room the group stood in.

"We are here. We exist. We were many, soon few. Find us. Help us. This message repeats."

Bastion stepped back. "Well, that's it then."

"What do you mean?" Larina asked.

Bastion didn't answer. He simply turned and stalked his way outside, his half-scarred face scowling.

"He now knows that Jorus was wrong," Onyx said.

"So this is our answer?" Creed accused. "This is our proof of a world beyond the Storm? How do we take this back to the tribes? This is what you were leading us to?"

"I told you," Onyx said. "To me, this place has been just rumor. I never knew one day I'd find it."

"This isn't a Stormwalker?" Aiden asked. "Maybe one of your people you didn't know of?"

Onyx shook his head. "This... person... we don't know. Not yet."

"Then what do we do with this?" Larina asked.

"This *is* proof of life out here," Onyx stated. "Or at least that there was. It's enough to keep going."

The Stormwalker left them then and followed Bastion out.

After Onyx left, Creed scowled. "We don't need proof that there *was* life out here. We need proof now!"

"And we'll find it!" Larina said. "Right Nemo?"

Nemo nodded hesitantly.

"I believe Onyx," Aiden said.

"Of course you do!" Creed laughed. "You've been the Stormwalker's little pet since we left."

"What do you think of this, Nemo?" Larina asked the girl. "Could this be from your people?"

Nemo watched the looping video for a moment and shook her head. "Not mine. Not Stormwalkers. Someone... else."

"So there *are* others out here, somewhere," Larina replied.

Creed didn't like it. "This machine. Every ruin I've ever scavenged has had them, but they've always been long dead. Why is this one going? Who's giving it life?"

"Maybe they come back?" Larina offered. "We could wait here until they come back."

"For how long?" Aiden countered. "Could be months. Or years. I say following Onyx is a better option."

Nemo continued to stare at the video.

"We are here. We exist. We were many, soon few. Find us. Help us. This message repeats."

She backed away from the screen then and shook her head. "No."

"Nemo?" Aiden asked. "What is it?"

"No. Can't trust them. Not them."

"Who are they?"

"Not us. Not Stormwalkers. Someone else. Can't trust."

"Like she says," Aiden confirmed. "I don't trust this thing. Onyx is the way."

Creed glared at the younger Pathfinder, but he saw the agreement in everyone else's eyes. They'd sided with the

Stormwalker already. "Great. So we keep blindly following the Stormwalker."

"Only until we reach Nemo's homeland. Then we follow her," Aiden said.

The others left Creed, who took a final look at the video.

"We are here. We exist. We were many, soon few. Find us. Help us. This message repeats."

Creed shook his head. "That's just great."

CHAPTER 32

The Storm transitioned again from biting cold to angry rainfall, and the harsh winds never stopped raging. The group trudged along a muddy hillside littered with fragments of buildings that jutted out of the dirt. They descended with care, slipping and shuffling, as they tried to avoid causing a mudslide down the steep hill.

Amidst the haze of rain around them, they found they had reached another ledge, a final steep drop to a vast and violent inlet of water that swelled below them. The remains of shipyard buildings and vessels had become scattered along the shoreline over the years of neglect and harsh weather.

Aiden pulled his rifle from his shoulder sling and aimed down at the scene below. He squinted and used the rifle's scope to get a better view and immediately spotted a faint light that glowed from within the window of a boathouse.

"There's someone down there," Aiden said.

The shipyard was a maze of boat skeletons that had rusted together long ago thanks to the Storm. The group made its way through the wreckage, chunks of metal and wood that provided shelter from the wind but also caused the rain to slice and fall at all angles. They paused behind a large upturned boat hull and watched the boathouse ahead. The glow in the building remained, seeping from various small portholes in the old building's walls. The light flickered as they peered at it.

"Could this be the land we seek?" Bastion asked no one in particular.

Creed shook his head. "We don't know if that's people in there. Could be more monsters like the others."

"Onyx," Aiden asked, "what are we looking at?"

The Stormwalker didn't answer, and when Aiden turned to Onyx to ask again, he found their guide was not present.

"Onyx?" Aiden called.

"Keep it down!" Creed hissed. "Whatever's in there might hear us."

"Where'd he go?" Bastion asked. "He was right here."

"Think he got scared?" Creed said. "Spooked by a light."

Larina shuddered. "Those tunnel monsters had lights."

Bastion wiped the dripping rain from his forehead. "What sort of people would live here? His people?"

"Whoever it is," Larina answered, "we should wait for Onyx."

"I guess waiting isn't your girl's strong suit," Creed said.

Aiden turned to see Nemo approaching the boathouse doors.

The rest followed Nemo, though much more cautiously than her. As they reached the door, she turned back to them with a big grin on her face. Then, before Aiden could stop her, Nemo grabbed the door and lurched it open a few inches. The door moaned and slid, letting a sliver of interior light pierce the hazy mist that surrounded them.

The group looked at the huddled silhouettes of Hobbes, Robin and Vic, who sat at a roaring campfire.

Hobbes turned to the group, smiling. "What took you guys so long?"

Creed, Bastion and Larina stood speechless.

Aiden's awe cracked, and he ran to his friend. He then engulfed Hobbes in an overly aggressive bear hug. The group was reunited once more.

Eventually Hobbes pushed Aiden away. "All right, all right. Wow, you guys are soaked."

Larina then shot forward and planted a hard kiss on Hobbes's face, practically knocking him over.

"Deal with it, you lucky bastard," Aiden laughed. "How the hell did you guys make it out of there?"

After Larina finally let him go, a blushing Hobbes nodded toward Vic. "Mostly thanks to the big guy over there. You might have had a Stormwalker, but we had our own big Dog. Wait, where is Onyx?"

As everyone settled around the fire, Aiden shook his head and smiled. "Right now I don't really care."

Steel girders lined the walls, and huge metal tracks ran the length of the ceiling, used long ago to move heavy ship components. In the dry docks rested several boats, rotted and collapsed, save for one. A fishing trawler built for short excursions sat on its own, its hull, deck and bridge seemingly in good shape. Aiden stared at the hundred footer and thought with a little work, maybe it would be seaworthy.

Maybe.

Aiden then noticed a flash of movement through the porthole window next to him. It was barely a glimpse, a shape moving through the dark amidst the shipyard debris. But its movements seemed inhuman, animal-like.

Then the large front doors opened slightly, and Onyx entered, startling Aiden.

"Don't scare me like that," Aiden said. "What were you doing out there?"

Onyx glanced to the group, who were mostly all asleep. "I can't stand snoring."

Aiden frowned. "You're a Stormwalker. You could stand a hurricane. Don't talk to me like I'm a child."

"You're right," Onyx agreed after a moment. "You're not a child. I see that now."

"Okay. Good," Aiden said. "My father rarely took me seriously, and if I'm supposed to lead my tribe out of here, then I can't have you doing the same."

"He was a fool."

That shocked Aiden. "What?"

"Your father. He was a fool to not see the courage in you, Aiden. If only he saw where you are now. I think you'll be all right."

Aiden seethed. "You gonna tell me what you were doing outside?"

"No."

Aiden shook his head and returned to the dozing group. He went to sit next to Hobbes, but paused when he noticed his friend had company. Larina sat at his side and the two of them playfully flicked small pebbles at Vic, who remained in a snoring slumber. As each pebble bounced off his face, he would halfheartedly swipe at nothing there. Hobbes and Larina stifled laughs.

Aiden was glad. Since his friend was occupied, he decided

to get some sleep himself and huddled down next to Nemo, who gracefully wrapped an arm around the young man. Content, Aiden swiftly fell asleep.

The following morning Vic found himself crammed into the small engine-room compartment of the remaining boat. Grease and oil covered him, but he worked feverishly on the engine. Robin appeared from the open hatch above him, carrying a bowl of steaming oats.

"Ahoy down there, ya scurvy Dog!" she called down to him.

Vic paused and looked up at her. "What'd you just call me?"

"Sailor talk," Robin sat and dangled her legs through the hatch. "Like from books."

"Never read 'em," Vic returned to his work. "Not much use for 'em, 'cept maybe to burn."

"I thought the Eagles kept thousands of books safe in their library."

"Mostly just the ones that fit what they preach, Robin," Vic wiped his hands with a rag. "The rest Jorus uses to wipe his ass with."

"Is that true, Bastion?" Robin asked.

Vic winced and looked up to see the young Eagle who stood there.

Bastion ignored the comment. "Jorus will need a lot more books for the Eagle library once everyone knows what is truly out here. Breakfast?"

Bastion handed his own bowl down to Vic, who sheepishly took it.

"Any progress?" Bastion asked.

Vic spoke with his mouth full. "Most of the cylinders are seized, but between both engines here we could run on the six good ones. Assuming I can start it by hand without the motor, it should be able to get us going. But is the hull watertight? That's another question."

Robin finished sipping from her bowl. "I didn't understand any of that."

An argument occurring from outside interrupted their conversation.

In the boathouse, Larina sorted supplies. Creed and Onyx stood nearby, face-to-face as each threatened to strike each other.

"But why not wait here?" Creed asked. "This building is strong enough to keep us safe until the Storm passes over. Let's stay!"

Larina carried a crate toward the boat. "Creed has a point, Onyx. You saw the bay out there. Why risk more than we need to?"

"I said I'd guide you through the Storm," Onyx stated, "not let you cower beneath it forever."

"We've fought off so much hell in this Storm!" Creed growled. "I'm getting sick of risking my life on this fool's quest."

Larina put the crate down. "You didn't call it a fool's quest when you volunteered, Creed."

"When I agreed to this, I thought we'd be getting out of all this mess. But Bastion was right! This Storm is a prison! And you, Onyx, are our jailer."

Onyx just stood there, his expression a void beneath his facial coverings.

"Don't ignore us, damn it! What aren't you telling us?"

Creed then shoved Onyx back against the side of the boat, but just as quickly Onyx wrapped his hand around Creed's throat. With an unnatural strength unknown to the rest of them, Onyx then lifted Creed, one-handed, into the air.

At that moment, Vic poked his head up from the boat hatch. "What's going on?"

Creed struggled, unable to speak, and grasped at Onyx's arm.

"I live in this Storm," the Stormwalker said. "I breathe its air. I drink its rain. I pass its tests. I survive because I am a part of it."

Creed began to turn blue when the boathouse doors groaned open, and the roar of the Storm rushed in. Aiden, Nemo, and Hobbes entered.

Aiden removed his face scarf. "That's the last of the debris cleared from the ramp, but I still can't figure how to get those launch doors open..."

Aiden then noticed Onyx holding the quickly suffocating Creed. But then Onyx dropped Creed, who collapsed to his knees and coughed. Onyx headed for the door and paused only briefly to acknowledge Nemo, who stood at the entrance. Then he was gone.

"What was that about?" Hobbes asked.

"I think the Storm is getting to us," Larina muttered.

Between coughs, Creed got to his feet. "Everyone we've lost is because of him."

"It's because of Onyx that we've even gotten this far," Aiden answered defiantly.

"He's right, actually," Bastion said as he exited the boat. "The ones we've lost were because of their own failures, not because of the Stormwalker. We owe him, and should heed his words."

"Creed sneered. "You'll follow anyone with an easy answer, won't you?" He then walked off as he rubbed his neck.

Vic, still partially hidden within the boat, cleared his throat. "Well, whenever you're all done bickering out there, maybe you should come and see this."

When they shuffled into the ship's engine room, they found Vic crouched next to the engine. He showed a large amount of gasoline that pooled on the floor around the engine. "See that?"

"Gas," Aiden muttered.

"A lot of it," Vic nodded. "As soon as I turned the pump on the chamber filled with it."

"What does that mean?"

"It means we now have the Storm's most flammable boat."

"So?" Hobbes said. "Have you seen the rain out there? No fire could burn out there."

Vic sighed. "It's no joke. All the rain in the sky won't help if this catches. Now I can patch the fuel line easy enough, but unless we find more gas, we ain't goin' nowhere. Maybe y'all could scavenge up some?"

"We'll see what we can find in the other wrecks," Aiden agreed. "Bastion, Hobbes-"

Hobbes moaned. "Awe man, we were just out there."

"Come on," Bastion said. "Let's get this done. But we should go in groups. Robin?"

"Sure!" Robin perked up. Then she looked to Vic. "I mean, if you're all right down here..."

"Better you than me, kid," Vic said as he went back to work. "You all know what you're looking for, yeah?"

"Sure," Robin grinned as she picked up an empty gas can. "Anything that smells like you."

Amidst the wreckage of the shipyard, it watched the four of them as they exited the boathouse. They fought against the torrential rain, not at all used to the weather's fury. But it didn't mind the rain. Not at all. It crouched, its shelled back providing built-in protection as it watched the pathetic people while they searched. Then, before chancing being spotted, it climbed over some wreckage and vanished from sight.

It's time had come.

CHAPTER 33

After the others left, Larina and Nemo slid the metal doors closed. Nemo looked worried.

"Hey, don't worry," Larina said. "They'll be back quick."

Nemo shook her head. "Not Aiden I worry for. Onyx."

"Nah, he's scary sometimes, but he's the one who got us this far. No one better built for the Storm than him, right?"

Nemo paused and searched for the right words. "Larina, you are strong. You survive. Aiden strong. Vic strong. But Onyx..."

"I don't understand. Onyx is strong."

"Stormwalker strong in Storm. But we are who he cares for. We are his weakness."

It perched in shadow. The others didn't see its tattered cloak as it whipped in the wind, blended with the torn sails of the many ship skeletons. As the group approached a rusted barge, the four of them split into pairs. Aiden and Hobbes tried to find a way to the upper deck while Bastion and Robin made their way into the ripped-open hull.

It made its choice, then followed.

Hobbes discovered a splintered cabin door, and together they wedged it open and slipped inside. They forced the door shut behind them to muffle the roar of the Storm outside. The ship itself rested on a slant, which caused them to make their way around at an odd angle.

As they pulled their goggles off, Hobbes flicked his flashlight on and looked around. "Can you imagine these things being out on open water? Look at the size of this one. Hard to imagine we let the weather get the better of us when we could build such things."

"That's why we call them the Stormmakers," Aiden replied. "They did this to themselves, and now we pay for it. Still, must have been nice back then. Not having to run with the Eye all the time."

Hobbes nodded. "Not having to scavenge for scraps."

"Not having to wear the same thing every day," Aiden smirked.

"Not having to eat anything you find," Hobbes added, "or always fighting each other."

"Something tells me they fought," Aiden said. He reached a console covered with layers of dust and gunk. As he swept the refuse away, he spotted a fuel gauge, which told him the reserve aboard was half full. "Hey, this says there's still gas in this thing. Finally, some luck!"

"Luck?" Hobbes scoffed. "We've relied too much on luck for this mission already."

"What you call luck, I call Onyx."

Hobbes's smile faded. "Where was the Stormwalker when the building fell on me? Where was he when Robin almost got eaten by a unicorn? He didn't stop us from losing Finch. Or Sparrow. Or Deacon..."

That stung Aiden. "Hobbes."

"Look, I owe him as much as anyone, but you gotta stop giving him credit for what we do. What we accomplish. Where is he now, huh? Where was he last night?"

"You think I don't believe in the group without him?"

"Larina, Robin, Creed, Vic, hell, even Bastion has pulled through despite being an Eagle nut job. And not because Onyx made it so."

"You forgot Nemo. She's the reason we're doing this."

"The reason we're risking our lives."

"Do you blame her for us leaving the Eye?"

Hobbes sighed. "No. No, I don't. It was the right call. This mission is important. We need a way out. It's just that as soon as she showed up then there was the Stormwalker. Then, before I knew it, we were on this crazy mission. I just wish we had more answers."

"She didn't speak our language, Hobbes. How could she answer?"

"She does fine now, yeah? Still no answers. You're the closest to her and she hasn't told you anything."

It was then Aiden's turn to sigh. "We're not there yet. Once she recognizes a way, then we'll get our answers."

They continued to inspect the cabin room and did not notice the sound of a metal rod being jammed into place against the cabin door. It tested the bar once, then it continued to the next target.

Bastion and Robin paused in awe as they entered the barge's hull. The interior was dark and cavernous. Although the ship rested at an angle, the floor had accumulated layers of mud and dirt over the ages that created a level but fragile surface to stand on. They began searching for fuel cans and other supplies.

"This boat is huge," Robin said.

"Yes, almost as big as Jorus's ego."

Robin glanced at the young Eagle in surprise. "Did you just make a joke about your boss? My, my, you've come a long way, Bastion."

"Jorus isn't my boss," Bastion stated. "He's my mentor."

"Well, he's just bossy to everyone else then."

"He gave me purpose when I had none," Bastion glared at her. "He did so for many people. It's why the Eagles are so big. People like control. Unity."

"Not the Birds. We have a leader, not a dictator. We've never needed someone who sees themselves as the 'Voice of the Storm'."

"Nothing wrong with giving people something to believe in," Bastion said, "or give them hope. We all have our messiahs. The group seems to think of the Stormwalker as one."

"They're not the same. Stormwalkers see themselves as part of the Storm."

"What about you?" Bastion asked. "Is there something you are part of?"

She almost laughed. "Don't even try. This girl ain't becoming an Eagle anytime soon."

"It won't be long before there'll be no choice. One banner. The Eagles. Strength in unity."

"I doubt that."

Bastion shook his head. "But it's already begun. Deacon's death and the failure of this quest will ensure it."

Robin halted her search and aimed her light on Bastion. "Failure? What makes you so sure we'll fail?"

Bastion squinted against her light and took a step toward her. "You actually thought we'd succeed? That's quaint. The Storm won't let us leave it. Best we can hope for is a safe return to the Eye and live with the Eagles in peace."

"What peace?" Robin asked. "There's always been fighting between the tribes. Always will be."

Bastion stepped forward again. "There is only one tribe, Robin. And if not yet, then soon."

Robin stepped back as horror built within her. "What do you know, Bastion? What's happened?"

He stepped closer to her. "By now Jorus will have given the Dogs an offer they wouldn't refuse. The Eagles and the Dogs have attacked the other tribes. War, Robin. All-out war. It's happening right now, if it's not already done."

"And you're okay with that?" she cried. "The others sure as hell won't be!"

Bastion sighed as he neared her. "Believe me, I-"

Bastion froze when he saw the shadow that loomed behind her.

Lighting crackled outside and illuminated the area for just a moment. But a moment was all Bastion needed to glimpse the nightmare that stalked them. Rags and wrappings covered it, similar to the way Onyx had. Strips of animal hide dangled from its arms and legs, trophies of its many kills. A tattered cloak hid its form, but the way it arched its back hinted at an animalistic monstrosity beneath. A dark hood covered its face. Red eyes provided a haunting glare from beneath the hood. In its clawed hands it clutched a broken piece of metal rebar.

"Robin, move!" Bastion ordered as he charged forward.

The instant Bastion moved, the creature leaped in the air. It measured its distance with great accuracy, for its descent aligned perfectly with the oncoming Bastion. It landed squarely on him, its feet slamming into his chest, which crumpled him down into the mud. The monster then spun to face Robin.

It charged her, rebar held high to strike. Then, just as it reached her, a gasping Bastion drew his pistol and fired three times. The first two shots went wide, but the third hit it in the shoulder and ricocheted off harmlessly. But the impact startled the thing, and it veered off and sprung back into the darkness.

In the cabin above, Aiden and Hobbes froze as they heard gunfire. Aiden rushed to the door but found it jammed shut from the outside. The metal bar did not budge.

Even through the Storm, Larina heard the gunshots. She grabbed her spear and ran for the door.

"Nemo, stay with Vic!"

Nemo stared after her.

Bastion shakily rose to his feet and reached Robin, but the damage was done. The piece of rebar had stuck at a slant through her torso. She just stood there and gripped the bar as blood seeped between her fingers. Finally she collapsed, but Bastion caught her and laid her down with care.

"Robin," he whispered. "Hold on, Robin..."

Robin spoke in an inaudible whisper. Her lips quivered, but no sound came through. Then Bastion brought his ear right to her mouth, and still he struggled to hear.

"Open your eyes," her rasping voice struggled, "see for yourself..."

He clasped her hand. "Hold on."

"Be your... own... man..." Robin winced.

Then she was gone.

Bastion lost himself then, as he slammed his fist into the mud and let out a roaring cry.

He then stood and waved his gun around. "Where are you? Where are you, monster! She didn't deserve that! Must the Storm claim another innocent?"

Out of the dark it lunged again. It collided with Bastion, and he tried to brace against the strike. But he was no match. The nimble beast body-slammed him into the mud again and gripped at his face. It pushed his head deep into the mud, and the ancient muck smothered his breath.

Bastion drowned in brown, runny earth.

Aiden and Hobbes took turns as they slammed against the door, to no avail. But then suddenly the door opened and Onyx was there, holding the metal bar that'd held the door shut.

"Onyx, what happened?" Aiden asked.

"Follow," the Stormwalker ordered.

His eyes and throat filled with mud, Bastion began to succumb to the suffocating mass of mud around him. But then the monster released him and dodged sideways as Larina's spear pierced the air it had just occupied. Bastion bolted up from the mud while he clutched at his throat and vomited mud.

Larina continued her attack on it as she relentlessly swiped and jabbed with her spear. Then she delivered a solid kick to its leg, which drove it to retreat into the dark once again.

Aidan, Hobbes, and Onyx arrived to find Larina kneeling beside Robin's body.

"Robin," Aiden whispered, then noticed the still-recovering Bastion. He marched directly to him and grabbed him by the collar. "What did you do, Bastion!"

Bastion could only gasp and cough.

"It wasn't him," Larina muttered.

"Then who?" Aiden dropped Bastion and glanced around. "Who else is here?"

Bastion finally caught his breath and sputtered out an answer. "The devil is real..."

Onyx watched the scene from the hull's open entrance when a bright-orange glow ignited from behind him, followed by a loud crack and boom.

The group turned as one to see the boathouse in the distance. It had been engulfed in flame. They witnessed the Storm's winds work to push the fire along, transforming it into a towering spiral of flames.

As the mountain of fire grew, reflected in Aiden's widened eyes, only one thought crossed his mind.

"Nemo," Aiden whispered.

CHAPTER 34

The boathouse was an inferno. The walls splintered and cracked as the flames licked their way toward the boat, Vic hurriedly closing hatches on the vessel. Nemo finished hauling the remaining supplies aboard just as the group fought their way inside. They dodged the creeping flames as they headed for the boat sitting above the water.

"Are you okay?" Aiden called to Nemo. He boarded the boat and handed Vic a couple containers of spare fuel they'd found.

"She's fine!" Vic cut in. "Help me get this boat on the water before we roast to death!"

Larina surveyed the burning debris all around them as she raced for the boat. "What happened?"

Her question got answered when Creed appeared from around the boat, an empty container in one hand. He casually maneuvered around the flames. "Fire. What do you think happened?"

"Who?" Hobbes asked.

As Creed boarded the ramp, Vic yanked the container from

him and tossed it aside. "Worry about that later! Get your asses up here!"

"The doors!" Aiden called. "They're closed!"

"Forget the doors!" Vic roared. "We'll bust through 'em! Just get up here!"

Finally, everyone climbed aboard. The rage of the flames grew nearer.

"Cut the lines!"

Bastion moved to do so, but also questioned Vic's orders. "Are you sure this boat will even sail?"

"We'll soon find out," Vic replied as he handed Bastion a hatchet, "but I'd start prayin' if I was you."

Bastion took the hatchet and ran to the bow. The others, meanwhile, scrambled to untie the last of the mooring lines.

"Last one!" Hobbes yelled as he struggled with an especially thick rope. Then he backed away as he saw Bastion approach.

Bastion raised the hatchet in the air. "Hold on to something!"

The hatchet crashed down upon the rope and severed it cleanly. Everyone braced for the slide down the boat ramp, but nothing happened save for a single loud creak.

Vic leaned out of the cabin window and pointed to a large winch at the far wall of the boathouse. "The anchor's still attached at that winch over there!"

But the boathouse continued to crumble down around them, the flames cutting them off from the winch entirely.

"Why didn't you release it first?" Creed accused. "No way to get to it now!"

Vic shook his fist. "I 'been busy fixin' this boat! What the hell you 'been doing all this time, huh?"

Larina then split their argument as she walked between them and pointed. "Look!"

The opposite wall of the boathouse had succumbed to the flames that lapped at it. It collapsed inward in parts, and at one of the newly created holes stood Onyx. He burst through and wasted no time in reaching the winch. He delivered a solid kick to it, and it released eagerly. The crank of the winch spun in a blur as the boat slid free and down the boat ramp, its speed enough to send the boat crashing through the still-closed dock doors. Twisted metal and flaming debris flew everywhere.

Once on the water, everyone scattered about the boat deck while Vic struggled to start the engine.

Aiden called back to the Stormwalker, who still stood inside next to the released winch. "Onyx! Come on!"

Then, in an incredible display of strength, speed and agility, Onyx ran over and through the burning rubble as it collapsed around him. The boat swiftly distanced itself from the boathouse as more and more water made its way between the boat and Onyx. But as Onyx reached the edge of the ramp, he swung around and delivered a spin-kick into a supporting beam. The beam instantly shattered free, and he forced it to collapse outward toward the water. As the beam fell, the group watched the Stormwalker mount the falling debris. Then with an inhuman display of balance he ran along the beam, and just as the end of the beam struck the water's surface, he launched himself up and forward in a jump they were sure no human could make. The group continued to stare amazed as Onyx landed squarely upon the boat's deck. He stood, unconcerned with the tiny licks of flame that singed at the fringes of his rags. Those small flames were then almost instantly snuffed out by the growing mists of sea air around them.

Larina, still winded and beaten from her fight with the intruder, got help from Hobbes and Nemo who guided her into the boat's small galley. They laid her on the table bench and glanced around, noting the few pots and pans that swayed from hooks and dishes that clinked in their shelving.

Creed soon followed them down. "Brave girl."

"Braver than you," Hobbes muttered.

"What was that?"

"Where were you?" Hobbes demanded. "You heard the gunfire and what, hid like a coward while she ran out to help? For years I thought you were a Pathfinder hero. A legend. You were always the brave one, like Deacon. You always went out on runs and brought back treasures. But out here, what have you done?"

"What have I done?" Creed scoffed. "What can I do? We're fighting a goddamn Storm! Not just the Dogs or some mutant fish!"

"Aren't we?" Hobbes pointed to Larina, "because she sure did."

"Whaddaya mean? What was it? What's out there?"

Bastion clambered down slowly into the room. "'And thou shalt look upon the face of evil. Unblinking eyes of flame.'" He ensured their full attention and spoke emphatically. "'And thine eye must never waver. Lest our lives never again be the same.'" He entered the group and crossed his arms, evidently still beaten from his encounter with the creature. "The Eagle library has books that spoke of such things. Ancient things. Things I didn't dare believe to be real. Made by man? Made by the Storm? They're not human. And the storm has sent one after us. We are not alone out here."

"So you *were* attacked," Creed confirmed.

"The demon took our most innocent like she was but a lamb."

Hobbes nodded. "Robin. Whatever it was, it killed Robin."

"I know what it was," Larina groaned, which caused everyone to turn and look to her. She propped herself up with Nemo's help. "I fought it, and I'm sure now. I don't know who he was, but he was definitely a man. He was human."

CHAPTER 35

Jorus sat at his own table and enjoyed his evening meal. He hummed lightly to himself. Ted stood nearby, bored but respectful. Jorus's humming got interrupted, however, when an Eagle scout burst in, clearly in distress.

"My lord!" the scout cried. "You better see this!"

Jorus held a finger up, which caused the scout to freeze in his tracks. Jorus finished chewing, patiently took a sip from his glass cup, and then wiped his mouth with a silk cloth. Finally, he stood. "Well?"

The scout led him to the tent entrance. Once he saw what the scout had been trying to tell him about, Jorus felt his blood run cold.

The Pathfinders and the Birds, gathered together as one, stood at the perimeter of the Eagle camp. They were armed, most with guns but many with whatever hand-held weapons they could muster; bats, clubs, knives.

"Bold move, Hawk," Jorus muttered.

"Pathfinders and Birds together," Ted said over Jorus's

shoulder. "This ain't good. And since you made Jonah take a Walk..."

"Isiah would have been easy to manipulate," Jorus finished.

"Bold, but stupid. Theodore, gather your Dogs."

Ted moved to follow the command, but paused as he spotted Isaiah at the front of the army signaling his people.

"Uh, too late!"

Isaiah raised his rifle high in the air. "Jorus' reign ends today! Attack!"

They charged.

From the Eagle camp poured a wave of enemies, a haphazard strike force made up of both Eagles and Dogs. Some Dogs were on their bikes, which bore down on the invading army.

"No hesitation!" Isaiah roared as he ran and fired his rifle at oncoming enemies.

Ted emerged from the camp upon his bike, and revving it, he gunned straight for Isaiah.

The two waves of enemies then met, and the hell of battle erupted upon the wasteland sands.

Gunfire echoed, and fighters fell. Fists and knives and pipes struck their targets, and blood pooled on the ground. Dogs, boldly riding upon their metal steeds, smashed their enemies with the sickening crunch of bodies beneath their wheels. Many roared in delight as they left their kills broken and alone in the dust.

Hawk and Canary stood back-to-back and fired at enemies that approached them. Dogs charged and fell, but more Dogs quickly replaced them. Canary risked a glance at her husband, a grim determination on her face. Hawk shared her look, and they fought on.

Isaiah and Reeves charged their way toward the camp. Reeves fired at every enemy that tried to block their way, and Isiah pressed on without stopping. He then saw Ted racing toward him and readied his own weapon. He saw the crazed grin on Ted's face. He knew he had to put an end to that look this day, whatever it took.

Barb and Ivy found themselves besieged on all sides by Dogs and Eagles. But they also fought with an expertize their enemies could not match. They cut every wave of attackers down by the swift strikes and long reach of the Thorns' spears. Bodies littered the surrounding ground, and still they did not stop.

Just as Ted reached Isaiah, he noticed the Thorns making short work of his men. Then, without veering from his true target, he whipped out his handgun and fired. A single *crack* of gunfire joined the multitude of others that sounded all around. In that same moment, Barb finished another sweep of her spear and slashed down three more Eagles. Her movement brought Ivy into her field of view, and seeing her best friend also strike down an enemy Dog, Barb also watched her suddenly falter and fall to a small explosion that erupted from her chest. Blood splashed into Barb's face as Ivy careened limply to the ground.

"No!" Barb screamed. She tried to go to her fallen friend, but the continued attack of enemies forced her to fight on.

Ted laughed and, joined by more Dogs, reached his actual target. Isaiah and Reeves faced the Dogs head on.

"Traitor!" Ted called to Reeves and opened fire. Isaiah and Doc Reeves split and ran while firing their own guns. They took down two Dogs but Ted did not stop.

Isaiah dove behind a pile of dead Eagles just in time to miss being clipped. Reeves, however, found no cover in his path. He gritted his teeth and twisted, firing the rest of his clip. Isaiah then watched his ally fall, the doctor's blank stare resting in his direction, a fresh hole in his forehead. Isaiah roared and, dropping his rifle, pulled out two handguns and rose from cover, unloading his shots blindly.

Hawk and Canary appeared beaten and bloody, but still standing. They saw Isaiah pinned down and alone, then checked their clips and faced each other.

"Ready?" Hawk asked his wife.

"Yes," she replied between gritted teeth. "I love you, Hawk."

Hawk pressed his forehead into Canary's and pulled her into a hug. He kissed her then, and the two faced their enemy. They charged.

Barb fought like an animal. Her spear claimed yet more enemies, but she also saw more waves of attackers pouring from the camp.

"Come on!" she screamed.

They did. She fought, but their numbers soon overwhelmed her. Then, finally, ragged and worn, she stared at the double barrel of a shotgun. She heard the blast, then nothing more.

Hawk noticed the movements of the Dogs and Eagles change, their gunfire leaving them as targets and finding their way to the lone Isaiah. Hawk paused then and took careful aim at the nearest bike.

The shot hit its mark, and the fuel tank instantly exploded in a ball of fire. The Dogs that didn't get consumed in the flames got thrown clear, Ted among them.

It relieved Isaiah when Canary joined him, handing him extra clips. He smiled grimly at her as he reloaded his guns.

Then, together, they again rose from cover and continued the fight.

Ted forced himself to his feet just in time to see Hawk barreling down upon him. Hawk dropped his gun in the sand and continued his charge.

"What's he doing?" Isaiah asked, watching the scene from their cover.

Canary watched her husband and nodded. "Teaching someone a lesson."

Ted and Hawk collided, and Hawk delivered a powerful uppercut to the Dog's jaw. Ted flew back and hit the ground again, hard. Hawk jumped on him and struck again and again.

Other enemies raced toward Hawk, but Isaiah and Canary, from their vantage point, chose their targets and fired, providing cover for Hawk to continue the job.

Ted's face was bloody and beaten to a pulp, but he finally caught one of Hawk's punches in his own palm. He held on and twisted Hawk's arm away in a lock.

"You think you're a man?" Ted asked through bloodied teeth as he whipped Hawk around to face the other way. He kicked the Bird leader in the back and sent Hawk falling flat on his face.

"Think you're a leader?" Ted continued as he tried to stomp on Hawk's head, but Hawk rolled just in time. "You got no idea what a leader is! What I done for my Dogs!"

Hawk rose and smirked. "All you did is help your Dogs die."

Ted glanced to the continued battle. He saw Canary and Isaiah still shooting many of his men and realized their attention had wavered from this fight. He subtly reached to his belt.

Hawk charged.

Ted swiftly retrieved a small blade, and as he continued with an underhanded flick of the wrist, he sent the throwing knife spinning at the oncoming Hawk. The metal stuck Hawk in the chest, and thanks to the Bird leader's momentum, caused the blade to sink in up to the hilt. Hawk stopped and looked down.

Taking down another pair of Eagles, Canary risked a glance to her husband just then. Her eyes widened as she saw Hawk lower to his knees. She tried to exit her cover, but returning fire kept her pinned in place.

Ted sauntered up to Hawk, who feebly grasped at the protruding blade with weakening fingers.

"Let me help ya with that," Ted smirked as he took hold of the knife and slid it out. Then he swiftly and silently stabbed Hawk again. And again. Hawk just sighed and then slumped over.

Ted spat on the lifeless Hawk and retreated behind his fellow Dogs. They made their way back to camp.

The decreased number of enemies finally allowed Canary and Isaiah to move to where Hawk remained. She kneeled next to her husband and pulled him into her arms. But Hawk had gone. She stifled her cries, kissed his forehead, and set him back down with great care.

Meanwhile, Isaiah witnessed many of their people falling in battle or being captured. The war was not in their favor. He turned back to Canary to find her marching alone toward the Eagle camp.

"Canary," Isaiah caught up to her. "Stop."

"Never," she growled. "That Dog is mine."

They reached the camp together just as four more Dogs emerged, but Isaiah and Canary made short work of them.

They entered the camp and approached the end of an ancient school bus parked in the way. They swiftly made their way around it only to find Ted waiting, a freshly gained handgun in each hand.

"Oops," Ted laughed. "Too bad."

They retreated around the bus just as Ted opened fire on them. Canary leaned out from cover to shoot back, but soon her gun clicked empty.

"I'm out," she muttered.

"I got a few," Isaiah assured her.

"Then cover me."

Canary raced back around the bus to charge Ted. The Dog leader drew his aim on her, but then Isaiah leaned out from cover and opened fire. Isaiah's efforts forced Ted to focus on him, which then allowed Canary to reach the Dog leader. He jumped at him and delivered a booted kick into his side. As he toppled back, she dove on him, and they wrestled in the dirt.

Ted delivered a few strikes, but Canary was quick. She spun and swept her leg out, kicking him again and again. Then, as he tried to crawl away in retreat, she scrambled over him and caught his neck in an armlock. She squeezed, hard.

"You think you're so strong!" she cried as she applied more pressure.

Ted gasped and twisted as he tried to get loose, but he couldn't pry her hold off his throat. Soon his windpipe got cut off completely.

"Try being a woman..." she cursed him.

Soon Ted gave a final pitiful gasp and died.

Canary kicked him aside as Isaiah reached her, and he helped her up.

"Finish this," she sighed as she tried to catch her breath.

Isaiah nodded and continued toward Jorus's tent. He passed a handful of wounded Eagles, but they did not stop him. Still, he gripped his gun tightly at his side.

Isaiah then rounded past a Jeep parked outside Jorus's tent. As he did so, Isaiah came face to face with a line of Eagles, all standing ready with rifles trained on him. Jorus stood just behind them.

The first Eagle fired, which struck Isaiah in the shoulder. Isaiah whipped around to the ground.

Canary heard the shot, and tried to race to the scene, but a group of Eagles rushed forward and restrained her. She tried to resist, but her fight with Ted had weakened her greatly. "No!"

Isaiah struggled to rise, but paused as a shadow loomed over him. He looked up to see Jorus.

"A noble effort," the Eagle leader said. He glanced a few meters away to the lifeless Ted. "Look at the mess you've made. Well, at least you saved me the trouble of doing it myself."

Jorus nodded and two Eagles forced Isaiah up, locking him in place to see Jorus face-to-face.

"Deacon. Jonah. Even the brat," Jorus continued. "Now you. This is becoming a hobby, ending the threat of the Pathfinders."

"We'll never surrender to you," Isaiah struggled.

Jorus laughed. "Look around."

They'd rounded up and restrained what remained of the Pathfinders and Birds. There were very few left, all being led away.

"They've already surrendered," Jorus continued.

"You gonna wipe us all out then?" Isaiah winced. "Well, get on with it."

"No, no. You have me all wrong," Jorus explained. "I won't

harm your people. You have my word. I'm not a monster. They get to live."

"They get to live *your* way," Isaiah muttered.

"Well, yes," Jorus nodded. "No more Pathfinder tribe. No Bird tribe. Just one tribe, the Eagles. They will live here, under my... guidance."

"For how long?" Isaiah asked. "Jonah told you about the Storm, I'm sure. Soon there'll be no land left. If I were you, I'd worry about that, not-"

"*You* don't get to do anything," Jorus interrupted. "I said that *they* get to live in my new world order."

Jorus approached Isaiah and drew out a curved knife from his robe.

"I never said *you* get to," Jorus stated, and then stabbed Isaiah once under his ribs. He then pulled away and watched the sputtering man. "Shhh. It'll be over soon. Just in time to watch your-, no, *my* people go away."

The two Eagles released Isaiah then, and he sank to his knees. He placed a hand against the wound and immediately drew it away, seeing the blood. He then looked to the battlefield and watched his people get led away. He saw Canary then, her hands tied, as they pulled her away with the others. He saw her futile struggle. He saw the tears in her eyes as they took her. Then she was gone.

Jorus leaned over and whispered in Isaiah's ear, "Say hello to Deacon for me."

Jorus left then, escorted by his Eagles.

Isaiah gasped, unable to speak. His eyes felt heavy, so he closed them. His head slowly lowered, his hands at his sides. Then, still on his knees, Isaiah drew his last breath.

CHAPTER 36

Waves crashed against the boat's hull. Onyx stood at the bow, watching the ribbon on his rifle barrel whip and dance in the wind. Aiden approached, clinging to the railing to keep his balance in the rough waters.

"Onyx!" Aiden called in the wind. "You should come inside!"

The Stormwalker did not respond.

"Why are you still out here?" Aiden continued as he approached.

Still no response.

"Onyx!"

"There," Onyx finally spoke, and showed the dancing ribbon. "You see it?"

Aiden stared at the flapping piece of cloth for a moment but did not understand. "See what?"

"The Storm is talking," Onyx said in awe. "She says we are close."

"She?" Aiden laughed. "The Storm is a She now, is She?"

Onyx was once again silent under his ever-unchanging masked face.

"So," Aiden continued. "You mean it? We're close?"

Onyx nodded. "The winds never lie. Soon we will be in uncharted lands. Nemo will have come from there, somewhere."

"Good," Aiden agreed. "Once she recognizes where we are, she'll lead us to her home. Then we'll have a route to bring the others out of the Eye. Will you come with us?"

"Undecided," the Stormwalker said.

Aiden changed the subject. "Vic just learned about Robin."

"Not taking it well?"

"We had to stop him from turning the boat around to go look for her," Aiden said, "or hunt down whatever-, whoever got her."

Onyx looked back out over the water. "I thought Dogs didn't care about anyone but themselves."

"My father used to tell me that too," Aiden said, "but this journey has taught me not to judge someone for the life they lived before. It's what you do now that matters. What we do for our future. Life is full of surprises, right?"

Onyx just stared at the young man for some time, then brought his hands to his goggles, as if to remove them.

But then the sound of sputtering machinery drew their attention, and they spotted large plumes of smoke rising through the hatch in the deck.

"No, no, no, no, no," Aiden cried. "The engine!"

Creed had been pacing back and forth in the galley for some time, appearing more and more anxious, a sheen of sweat plastered over him, when the engine blew.

"What the hell was that?" he cried. "What's gone wrong now?"

The others, who sat at the table, also rose to the sound.

"Engine trouble?" Bastion asked.

Creed glanced around wildly, his sweat running off him in torrents. Hobbes noticed and approached with reassurance.

"Creed, it's all right. Calm down."

"Calm down?" Creed's eyes widened even more. "This is no time to be calm! Maybe if I were back home in the Eye where we all belong, then I could be calm!"

As he shouted, Nemo entered the room with caution. She heard the commotion and approached the frightened Creed from behind.

"But no!" Creed continued. "Instead, I'm stuck who knows where on a broken boat with a bunch of maniacs who actually think they can get through this!"

Nemo stood directly behind Creed, hands on her hips. "You the maniac."

Creed whirled around to face her. As he did, one hand reached into his tunic and withdrew a small pistol. She saw it and immediately tried to retreat, but Creed swung his free hand out and grabbed her by the hair. He held her in place and butted the barrel of the gun against her temple.

"There she goes again," Creed scowled, "running her little mouth."

"Creed," Hobbes almost whispered. "What're you doing?"

"Leave her alone!" Larina demanded.

Creed tugged Nemo toward him, making her his hostage. "I know you can speak just fine, you little bitch. Now start talking!"

"For your own sake," Bastion said, "Stop this."

Creed laughed. "You're all mad! What'll it take for you all to see that this is suicide? Hobbes, you know me, yes?"

"I thought I did," Hobbes muttered.

"You said you looked up to me, once," Creed continued. "Can't you see what I've done was to protect us? To convince you all to turn back?"

Hobbes didn't understand. "What you've done?"

As Nemo struggled against Creed's grip, she got out a single word. "Fire."

"Shut up!" Creed barked as he jerked her around.

"She said fire," Larina growled and approached, "Creed set the boathouse on fire!"

Panicked and confused at their reactions, Creed stepped back while dragging Nemo with him.

"Why?" Hobbes pleaded.

"No boat, no way further," Creed stated plainly, "forced to turn back. Can you honestly say you don't want to go home?"

Everyone remained silent.

"You see?" Creed demanded as he adjusted the gun barrel against Nemo's temple. "It's up to me then."

He suddenly dragged Nemo back and up the narrow stairwell toward the bridge. The others followed at a careful distance.

Out on the deck, Aiden reached down and opened the engine-room hatch. A plume of thick smoke escaped out and into the wind, which forced Aiden to cough and cover his eyes as he peered inside.

"If we have a fire down there, the whole boat could blow," Aiden called back to Onyx. "Best get Vic to-"

Suddenly the beast was there as it launched itself out from the smoke-filled hatch, its taloned hands taking hold of Aiden and dragging him with it. The beast tumbled across the deck and came to a stop at the edge of the boat, as it grasped Aiden in one hand.

Onyx followed the commotion to find Aiden dangling out over the open water like bait, held aloft only by the beast's firm grip on his throat.

"No!" Onyx cried in uncharacteristic horror. "Stop!"

The beast halted and turned its face to look at the Stormwalker. As Aiden struggled against his captor's grip, he finally got a good look of the creature, only to discover it wasn't a creature at all. The beast was a man, clad in the familiar garb of the Stormwalkers, but with differences. Instead of goggles, this Stormwalker wore a full gas mask, white and flat, folded with a grill where the mouth would be, and red lenses hid the man's actual eyes beneath. Under his hooded cloak, his back had a large shell strapped to it. Thick leather wrapped his hands, creating bracers with sharpened metal talons on the ends of his fingers; fake, but still lethal. Braids and ribbons tied all over gave the appearance of fur, but he was just a man. But his grip on Aiden proved he was an incredibly strong man.

"Skarn," Onyx almost pleaded. "Don't do it."

The beast called Skarn looked back to Aiden and chuckled. A muffled voice emanated from behind the mask. "This is him, isn't it?"

Onyx cautiously approached. "Leave him be."

"This is the one you left us for?" Skarn hissed. "You chose weak little Eye-dwellers over your own? After we let you in?"

Onyx took another careful step forward. "I chose to lead them out. Let me finish my mission."

With a slight flick of his clawed hand, Skarn sliced a crimson gash across Aiden's exposed forearm. Aiden hissed in surprised pain and watched as his blood dripped into the water below his dangling feet.

"A little blood in the water is all I need," Skarn said.

"Damn it, Skarn," Onyx cried. "This is not the way!"

Onyx took another step forward, but Skarn leaned further out, the pained and struggling Aiden hanging further over the water. Onyx backed off.

"Are you not afraid of the Stormwalkers, boy?" Skarn asked the young Pathfinder. "Do you think we are your friends?"

With his free hand, Skarn grasped the edge of his mask. He pulled it aside and revealed to Aiden a mutated face beneath. Gnarled muscle was exposed within caved-in cheekbones. A wild abandon filled blood-shot eyes. A sinister grin of sharpened teeth snarled beneath the cavity where no nose was to be found.

"We are not," Skarn muttered through cracked lips, then slid the mask back into place. He then tossed Aiden overboard.

"No!" Onyx roared and charged Skarn.

The two Stormwalkers collided, and Onyx savagely pummeled his fellow nomad. Skarn, however, seemed barely fazed by the blows.

Vic frantically muddled through the wires under the main steering controls. Busy in his task, he didn't notice as Creed emerged from below, Nemo in his grip, and the two of them soon followed by Bastion, Hobbes and Larina.

"Victor!" Creed shouted. "Time to turn this boat around!"

Buried under the control wiring, Vic was oblivious to the hostage situation. "If you haven't noticed, we are dead in the water! So until I figure out what's wrong with this blasted thing-"

"I said turn this boat around and head back to shore!" Creed barked.

Vic then crawled out from under the control panel. "Listen, dumb ass. If you yell orders at me like that again-" Vic then finally saw the gun held to Nemo's head. "Creed? The hell you doing?"

"What I have to do to get us home. Now take us back!"

Vic shared a look with the others and noticed as Bastion subtly shook his head. "I can't do that, Creed. The engine is down and we can't exactly paddle through the Storm, can we?"

Creed yelled and threatened to shoot Nemo then.

Instead of plunging into the cold waters below, during his fall Aiden took hold of loose mooring lines that dangled off the side of the boat. He struggled to hang on as the waves battered him again and again and forced himself to climb back to the deck above. He brought one hand up and grasped the ledge of the deck when a deep hissing noise cut through the rain and wind behind him. He turned and stared in fear as a huge ribbed fin snaked its way through the water toward the boat.

Onyx and Skarn paused their fight when a second loud hissing noise echoed from out in the water.

"Ah, that didn't take long," Skarn said with satisfaction.

Onyx stared at the former Stormwalker ally he'd been punching. "What have you done?"

Then Skarn kneed Onyx in the ribs, which drove the taller Stormwalker off of him. As Onyx rolled away, Skarn leaped up and took hold of him, dragging him across the deck. He wheezed from behind his mask, "I'm ending your little experiment."

Creed was frantic. "You can fix it! You're a Dog! That's what you do! So do it!"

Vic held back his anger, but stood firm.

"Fine," Creed growled. "Then I'll see my own way back."

While Nemo struggled against the gun still pressed to her head, Creed reached for the nearest wall. There he flipped open a mounted box labeled RAFT and pulled out a yellow heap of rubber in his hand. A small flare gun toppled from the box and clattered to the floor in the center of the room.

"Creed," Bastion tried to reason, "think about what you're doing."

As the situation unfolded, Hobbes found his attention drawn to the bridge's windows. "Uh, guys? What's going on out there?"

They could all see outside, amidst the crashing wind and rain, the two forms of the Stormwalkers, Skarn raising Onyx into the air above him.

"It can't be," Bastion whispered.

Then Skarn tossed Onyx through the windows. The taller Stormwalker smashed through the glass and forced everyone to take cover. The weather also rushed in and turned everything into chaos.

It was the distraction Nemo needed. She lowered her head forward, then swung it back up, the back of her skull smacking into Creed's face. Creed staggered back in surprised pain, and before he brought his gun to bear on her, Nemo spun and delivered an abnormally powerful kick, which sent him back out through the bridge door.

As he skidded backward, Creed fired off a single shot of his gun. Everyone jumped, but it was Bastion who found himself with a large opening in his gut as he dropped to his knees.

As Creed hit the deck, he released the packaged life raft.

The yellow bundle slid along the deck's surface as the boat rocked back and forth upon the waves.

Creed struggled to his feet and looked back at the bridge with everyone still inside. Some were tending to the fallen Onyx. Creed sneered and raised his gun, drawing a bead on Nemo again. But before he took the shot, a hand startled him, grabbing his leg and sweeping him back down to the deck. He then stared face-to-face with Aiden, who finally rose to the deck.

Aiden was furious. "What are you doing?"

"No more, Aiden!" Creed screamed. "You're all crazy! Everything out here is trying to kill us!"

Aiden shook his head. "Including you."

Creed's expression stiffened, and he aimed his gun at Aiden.

The loud hissing sound returned. It drew both their attention as they looked down into the dark waters below.

The sea then rose before them, a monstrous set of jaws lunging in their direction. The two scrambled back into the bridge as a massive animal bludgeoned its way aboard their vessel. It was a huge reptile, its long form sporting the great ribbed fin seen from the water. The fin ran the length of its back and long tail. Row after row of large, serrated teeth lined its huge snout. Its stubby legs thrashed for purchase on the boat's slippery deck, its sheer size causing the whole vessel to teeter in its direction.

The group clung to whatever they could as the boat continued to tip. The snapping jaws of the crocodilian creature waited just beyond the bridge's open door below them. Larina and a wounded Bastion clung to the unconscious Onyx, stopping him from sliding to a gruesome death.

With one hand gripping for dear life, Creed used his free hand to fire his pistol frantically at the reptilian giant. He emptied the clip, but the bullet strikes did little to dissuade the monster.

During the chaos, Vic spotted the flare gun. He reached and just grabbed it, and, eyes squinted, he fired a blinding red shot right into the monster's mouth. The beast reared back and released its grip on the boat, which sent everything and everyone rocking back upright. The giant croc then crashed back into the waters and vanished beneath the waves.

Bastion released Onyx then and grimaced at his bleeding wound.

"He's hurt bad!" Larina noticed.

"The hell just tried to eat us?" Hobbes demanded.

Creed shivered and clutched his empty gun. "What if it comes back?"

"Then we feed you to it!" Vic growled, "and hope it dies from food poisoning."

"Onyx!" Nemo shook the Stormwalker. "Onyx, wake up!"

"There's another one out there," Aiden muttered as he got to his feet.

"What?" Creed exclaimed. "Another monster?"

Aiden shook his head. "Another Stormwalker. I'm sure he's the one that killed Robin."

Vic's eyes narrowed. "Then he and I have business."

"Vic, wait," Aiden tried to hold the Dog back. "He's strong. Really strong. Look what he did to Onyx."

"Then good thing I'm strong too," Vic replied as he went to the life raft box and rummaged through it. He came away with a handful of flare shells and reloaded the flare gun. "Just need to get close, and I'll light that bastard up!"

"Guys," Larina said again, "Bastion needs help!"

"Better start praying, Eagle," Creed muttered.

Hobbes shook his fist at Creed. "You'll start praying if you know what's good-"

The bridge shifted then as the boat rocked far onto one side.

"That thing must have torn up the hull," Aiden interjected. "I think we're taking on water."

"Great!" Creed screamed.

"The life raft!" Hobbes realized. "Creed, where's the life raft?"

"How should I know? I lost it when that monster showed up!"

"Raft," Nemo said, and the group looked to where she pointed.

Their hearts sank.

The bundled life raft sat at the feet of Skarn, who stood watching the group. The rain bounced off his hood, the lenses of his mask reflecting each arc of distant lightning.

Vic clicked the flare gun closed. "I got this."

"Wait Vic, we go too. Larina, Nemo, stay with-" Aiden paused as Larina glared at him and shook her head. The Thorn woman gripped her spear tightly. Aiden nodded. "Nemo, help Onyx and Bastion. The rest of us will bring this bastard down."

That time Larina nodded.

The group emerged from the bridge to confront Skarn. The Stormwalker stood his ground and allowed the life raft bundle to slide back and forth on the deck with the rocking of the sea. He teased them with their needed prize.

"Why are you doing this?" Aiden asked, only to receive a

deep, mocking laughter that echoed out at them. "Why are you so determined to make us fail?"

His laughing dwindled, and he removed his mask to reveal the twisted face beneath.

"Because the world has no place for you anymore," Skarn rasped. "Everything evolves, except you. You and your tribes are as good as extinct animals."

"Yeah?" Vic responded and lifted the flare gun. "Well, this extinct animal has a gun."

But before he pulled the trigger, the monster croc was upon them again, launching itself onto the deck once more. It forced its way aboard even further this time, great claws shredding the hull of the boat as it went. The vessel violently tilted and shook, scattering everyone and causing Vic to drop the flare gun again. He watched helplessly as the gun slid along the deck and into the open hatch of the engine room.

Though the beast attempted to snap up whoever it could in its massive jaws, it proved to be fairly clumsy out of the water. Hobbes narrowly ducked under its tail as the huge appendage swept across the deck, shearing off the roof of the bridge. Nemo and Bastion huddled over the still-prone Onyx as the surrounding bridge collapsed. Larina, spotting the life raft, scrambled toward it. She reached it just in time to get pinned to the ground as Skarn stamped down on her back.

"I know how to swim these waters. Do you?" Skarn asked Larina. He reached for her, but then Vic collided with him from behind, driving him off of her.

"You owe me a life!" Vic roared.

Skarn's crooked face smiled back at Vic, barely fazed by the Dog's hit.

The croc continued its hunt, chomping and biting at the

many targets that fled around it. In the confusion, Creed spotted an opportunity and took a running slide past the reptile. As he neared the engine-room hatch, he dove inside and out of sight.

Nemo and Bastion struggled out of the debris of the bridge, Onyx slung over their shoulders. Hobbes ran to help, but the croc intersected them and went in for the multi-target kill. They dodged in time and the croc lumbered past them, scooping up the ship's wheel into its jaws, thrashing its snout back and forth. The violent thrashes connected with them, and Nemo, Onyx and Hobbes were sent hurtling into the sea. Bastion barely avoided the strike and dropped beneath the beast, clutching his wound with one hand, crawling with the other. Larina, no longer troubled by Skarn, scrambled and took hold of the life raft.

"No!" Aiden cried as his friends went overboard. He ran after them. On the way, Larina intersected him.

"Raft!" she shouted, tossing it to him. He caught it and dove overboard. She then reached the edge of the deck, looking back at Vic.

He held Skarn at bay, clenching his fists in anticipation. "Go!" he yelled back to her, then charged the Stormwalker.

Larina leaped from the boat.

The rough sea proved difficult for Aiden to swim in, but as he kept looking ahead at his friends in peril, he strengthened his resolve. He soon reached them, and, fumbling with the cord, he made the raft inflate into a large yellow hexagon. Larina arrived then and helped get them into the raft.

Once aboard, Hobbes looked around and coughed. "Where's Bastion?"

Back aboard the boat, Bastion forced himself to his feet. His gunshot wound was bleeding out. He couldn't stop it. He glanced across the bridge to see Vic and Skarn fighting. He took a step toward them, but then glanced back at the croc. The great beast had just finished chomping on the ship's wheel, and was looking out across the water at the life raft, a bright-yellow spot in the black waters.

"Hey!" Bastion yelled, waving his arms. He knew the croc's intent and wasn't about to let it happen. Despite bleeding out, he charged the monster. "Hey! Leave them alone and face me, monster!"

The croc turned to face him, and he quickly veered toward Vic and Skarn. The croc followed.

Vic punched Skarn in the face, yet another in a long succession of strikes, but still the Stormwalker just grinned. Skarn then delivered a swift knee to Vic's gut, downing the larger man instantly.

"Primitive," Skarn said. "You can't beat me."

Skarn then turned just in time to face the approaching Bastion.

"Vic, run!" Bastion yelled. The young Eagle struck out with a weakened attack, but Skarn was quick to dispatch him. Skarn spun and with both hands shoved Bastion, sending him careening past Vic and through the open engine hatch.

Lying on the deck, Vic watched as Bastion fell from sight. He also watched Skarn follow the Eagle and took it as his cue. Reaching into his jacket, his hand withdrew, clutching the rest of the Narwhal horn. Vic jumped up and lunged at the Stormwalker, causing Skarn to turn back to him. Just as he did, Vic plunged the horn deep into his thigh muscle.

"Gotta make it right," Vic wheezed.

Skarn screamed in agony as he fumbled at his impaled leg.

His pained cry faltered, however, when he noticed the croc bearing down on them. The giant reptile rounded the pile of debris that was once the bridge, and, spotting Skarn, charged directly at him. Skarn hobbled away but was then stopped as Vic latched his mighty arms around the Stormwalker. Skarn struggled, but his wound had weakened him. Vic's grip was too strong.

"That's for Robin!" Vic shouted and laughed as the croc arrived. Then, as one, they were both snapped up in the monster's jaws.

Smoke filled the engine-room, and gas flooded the area ankle-deep. Bastion groaned and rose to his knees, only to find Creed standing before him, flare gun pointed in his face.

"Get out of here!" Creed exclaimed. "You're bleeding everywhere, you'll attract that thing!"

"Well, whose fault is that?" Bastion coughed.

"I mean it, Bastion! I won't die for your cause!"

"My cause is the same as yours!" Bastion said as he struggled to his feet, no longer caring about the flare gun. "We're on the same side. What's wrong with you?"

"This whole mission is pointless! There's nothing out here but death. You see what 'rewards' your faith provides? Jorus, Onyx, Deacon—, they're all just as bad. They all sent us to die."

"This is bigger than them, Creed," Bastion reasoned. "Bigger than us. I've spent my whole life in the Eye listening to Jorus and know what I've learned? That out here I don't have to listen. I'm so far from where we started that all I hear is the sound of my voice and the power it has." He regarded the surrounding room in the sinking ship. "So what if we don't make it back? We have seen wonders on this expedition that rival lifetimes in the Eye."

Creed faltered for a moment.

"Now do we sink, trapped in the ship like we've been trapped all our lives," Bastion finished, "or do we push on and help our friends?"

Creed pondered his words. He began to hand the flare gun to Bastion when the snout of the croc suddenly smashed its way into the hatch, forcing both of them to scramble back on the floor, sloshing around in the gas.

The croc continued to reach for them, but it soon realized they were just too far in. It returned its attention to the yellow raft on the water and headed back to the sea.

In the confusion, Bastion wrestled the gun from Creed's grasp. He then headed back up the ladder, leaving Creed to cower in the dark. Crawling halfway out of the hatch, Bastion took aim at the slowly retreating croc. But before he could fire, he felt hands on his ankles and Creed violently yanked him back down into the engine room. His head smashed on the rungs of the ladder as he fell, ending in another splash of gasoline below.

"What are you doing?" the delirious Creed demanded. "You'll bring it back here!"

Bastion rubbed his head, coughing out gas he'd swallowed. "It'll go after the others if we don't stop it."

Creed pinned Bastion's arms behind him and reached for the flare gun. "You can't stop something like that with a flare, Bastion!"

Bastion reared back and smashed Creed into the ladder, but Creed kept his hold. Bastion then regarded the pool of gas flowing around them.

"You're right," Bastion said as he aimed the flare gun at the floor.

Creed panicked. "What are you doing? Is this what your Stormgod would want?"

Bastion exhaled. "Let's go ask Him."

Bastion then closed his eyes and pulled the trigger.

The croc fumbled halfway over the deck into the sea when the boat erupted into a massive fireball, sending much of the beast into the sky in a rain of blood and charred flesh.

Aiden, Nemo, Hobbes, Larina and Onyx held on for their lives as the explosion rocked and pummeled the life raft. Then, without knowledge of where they were, the group watched helplessly as the sea carried them away.

CHAPTER 37

Jorus stood amidst the charts and graphs once studied by Jonah and Deacon, smirking at his intrusion of their former Pathfinder home. He held a burning candle in one hand as he noted the pair of drink cups abandoned on the table.

As he approached the pinned-down charts, he traced his finger along the routes penciled over and over across the aged parchments. His route continued for some time until his finger came to a pause at the drawn coastline.

He turned, going to another map pinned to the wall. He repeated the tracing action and again came to the coastline. Panicking, he went to a third chart, but the outcome was the same.

Jorus paused. Moving to Jonah's chair, he sat and exhaled a deep sigh.

He had promised to take the remaining Pathfinders under his wing, to give them a hope and a purpose. They would be Eagles, but they would have lives. But for how long?

He had fought them for so long. He opposed their methods,

denied their beliefs, condemned their warnings. But the tribes had been right. The Pathfinders had always been right. The Eye would reach the coastline, and it would trap them.

They were out of time.

Jorus glanced around the room once more; the charts, the forgotten cups, little knick-knacks littered about. They belonged to no one now. Finally, his eyes paused on a Stormwalker doll laying on the bed where Nemo had once rested.

Jorus went to the doll, examining it in one hand for a moment. He then returned to the table of charts and placed his candle next to a map, letting the flame take hold of the map's corner. He watched as the fire slowly but surely crept along the map's edge, connecting to another map, and another. He then turned and went to a shelf of rolled-up charts and lit them ablaze too.

The growing glow of the creeping fires slowly overcame the night's darkness.

Jorus exited the tanker and watched as the fire soon swallowed the vehicle in an inferno. As the blaze reflected in his eyes, Jorus remembered that he still held the doll in hand. He examined it once more.

"You win, Stormwalker," Jorus muttered. He then unceremoniously chucked the doll into the growing wildfire. He motioned for his entourage of Eagles, who had waited for him outside, to depart.

As they exited, the fire had traveled from the tanker to its neighboring tent, then the following car, and so on.

The fire grew and grew as it consumed everything, all evidence of the camp lost in the flames.

The Pathfinders were no more.

R.K. KING

Jorus did not look back.

CHAPTER 38

Gentle waves lapped at the shore of a peaceful beach. Debris littered the sand, along with the unconscious forms of Aiden and Nemo.

Nemo soon awoke and forced herself up. She took in their surroundings and kneeled next to Aiden.

"Aiden," she whispered, gently shaking him. He groaned, but awoke.

"Nemo?" he asked, looking around. "Where are we?"

Aiden attempted to stand, stumbled a bit, and regained his balance. He and Nemo leaned against each other for support as they continued to look around.

They were on the shore of a once-popular tourist beach. Dilapidated hotels and condo buildings lined the shore in the distance, facing the ocean. Rusted vehicles stood a silent vigil up and down the cracked streets. Amidst the overgrown vegetation they spotted a rotted and paint-stripped sign; COCOA BEACH.

Despite the obvious signs of previous life, Aiden found himself more surprised at how calm the weather was.

This was it. They had made it through the Storm.

"We did it. We really did it," Aiden smiled at Nemo's enthusiastic nods. "Hobbes, we-"

Aiden looked around again, realizing that Hobbes, Larina and Onyx were nowhere to be found. Nemo looked solemn.

"Wait," Aiden started. "Where are-"

"Aiden," Nemo shook her head.

"Hobbes!"

"Aiden..."

Aiden walked, Nemo following closely.

"Hobbes!" he cried. "Larina!"

"Aiden, stop."

"Onyx!"

Finally she grabbed his shoulders, turning him to face her. "They're gone."

"No," Aiden was adamant. "No, they're not."

"Yes."

Aiden paced back and forth. "We made it. We made it! After everything we've faced, we're still here!"

"We are."

"So they are too!" he reasoned. "They've gotta be!"

"But they're not."

"We gotta look for them!"

"Aiden, we have to go."

"No! I'm done running! We're here now!"

"We're not there yet. I think I know where we are. We finally on the right track. We can make it, if we go now."

Aiden marched off again. "Help me find them!"

"Stop!"

He did, wheeling around to face her. "Why? Why aren't you helping?"

"They not here," she replied. "We can't help. So we go. Now."

"I can't lose them now," Aiden muttered as he looked out to the open ocean. "Not after all this. Hobbes never wanted to be part of this. He came to watch out for me. Now he's gone. And Deacon's gone. And I doubt we'll ever see the Pathfinders again..."

"Aiden..."

"No," he said, looking back at her. "We trusted in you. We trusted Onyx. We gave up our lives in the Eye, hoping for something better. Well, here it is. And who gets to enjoy it? Us. Just us. I've lost everyone."

"You have me."

"That's not enough, Nemo," Aiden sighed. "Not this time."

"What you mean?"

"Everyone that has died. Everyone that will die within the Eye. I think of how life was before we found you."

"You regret finding me?"

Aiden nodded slowly.

Nemo backed away. "Well, I don't regret. Not one bit. 'Cause I love Aiden..."

Tears forming in her eyes, she turned and rushed away.

"Nemo, wait," Aiden said, but she didn't listen. He chased after her, finding it hard to keep pace. She gained speed as she turned around the corner of a building. As he followed around the same corner, he paused. He could see ahead for a long stretch, but he couldn't see her.

Nemo was gone. Aiden was alone.

"Nemo!" Aiden called. "I'm sorry!"

The first thing Hobbes saw when he awoke was an intense yellow glow. He panicked and clawed at the heavy yellow plastic that was the deflated life raft, the morning sun shining weakly through it. Finally, he pulled himself from beneath it and blinked at the real morning sun.

The shore was sunny and calm. The water reflected the bright-blue sky above. Green trees and other foliage lined the beach, casting long shadows over the sand. Across the water in the far distance was the massive dark swirling of the Storm Wall.

Hobbes sat up. Confused and unbelieving, he spotted Larina standing at the water's edge; the waves washing over her feet as she wiggled her now-bare toes in the wet sand. She watched the distant Storm Wall.

Hobbes stumbled over to join her. "Larina?"

"We made it," she said, smiling. She pointed to the Storm Wall. "Look. We're beyond its walls."

Hobbes looked down to his feet, where a small crab scuttled past in the water. "Is this for real?"

Larina delivered a sharp punch to Hobbes's shoulder.

"Ow!"

"That feel real enough?"

"Yeah! It did!"

"Good," she grinned and wrapped her arms around him in a tight hug. Hobbes happily held her for a moment, but then his face expression soon turned to one of concern.

"Wait, where are the others?"

Larina released him. "It was just us when I awoke. You, me and the raft."

"Where could they have gone?" Hobbes wondered. "Aiden!"

"I don't see any other tracks in the sand. Maybe they came ashore somewhere else."

Hobbes took a few steps into the water. "What if they're still out there? What if- "

"They have Onyx with them," Larina reasoned weakly. "He's more than capable. I'm sure we just got separated. That's all."

She took his hand and led him back to the sand. "Come on. I bet they are the ones thinking we didn't make it. They're probably looking for us right now."

"Yeah," Hobbes reluctantly agreed. "Yeah, okay, you're right."

"Remember, we thought we lost you in the snow, but you surprised us all, right? This'll be the same, I'm sure."

Hobbes nodded. "Well, where do we go from here?"

"We go someplace that stands out," Larina said. "Somewhere they wouldn't ignore."

Hobbes tilted his head and looked past Larina. "Somewhere like that?"

Larina turned to see a massive gray-and-white building in the distance rising above the treeline. The highest structure in the area, it was square, its metal surface gleaming in the morning sun like a great beacon. A large, circular blue logo was on one side, but the wear of weather and time made it hard to decipher, especially at their distance.

"Perfect," Larina nodded.

Aiden wandered alone.

He could hear the calm waves as they hit the shore and the

squawking and chirping of birds as they flew overhead. He'd never seen so many free birds.

He tried to find signs of where Nemo went, but the area seemed empty of anyone. Just him.

Aiden eventually came upon a long pier that jutted far out into the water. He stepped upon it, passing a run down building at its entrance.

The place had once been some kind of food service business, not unlike some kiosks at the market back in the Eye. But now crabs and other sea life made it their home. He looked over the various touristy items left behind, even deciphering an old menu. He looked in the windows but it was too dark within; the view blocked by upturned tables and other debris. The place had once teemed with life, but like everything else, it had died away.

He continued to the end of the pier. He reached the end railing and leaned on it, looking out over the vast open water. The Storm Wall still swirled violently in the distance, but seemed to be foreign to the world Aiden was now in.

"It's beautiful," the familiar voice said from behind him. He instantly turned to find Nemo, who fidgeted slightly. "The ocean."

"Yeah," Aiden said.

They stared at each other, silent, as a light shimmer of rain began to fall around them. Barely more than a mist, it was just enough to dampen their hair. Aiden noticed Nemo's skin glisten against the sheen of water that connected to them and reached forward to wipe some accumulating rain from her forehead.

"I'm sorry," Aiden sighed.

"I know."

"No, really," Aiden said. "You didn't deserve that."

"You not wrong. We lose many."

"But that's not your fault. For finding you, I'm grateful."

The rain increased a little then, and Aiden took action. With a display of effort, he went to the abandoned restaurant and forced the door open. It resisted at first, to his dismay. His chivalrous act threatened to be compromised, but then the door finally relented. He got it open and turned back to her, slightly embarrassed.

She just stared, smiling warmly.

They entered the restaurant just as the rain came to a head, not anything like the Storms they'd fought through, but enough to keep warm from.

Aiden got the door closed just as her hand grasped his shoulder. He turned to face her and saw the look she was giving. Her face was flushed. She bit at her lip and shuffled on her feet slightly.

She surprised him then with a kiss. And as he heard the sounds of rain on the roof and the distant rolling of thunder fade away, Aiden became lost in another world.

A world for two. A world for him and her. Aiden and Nemo.

"Nemo," Aiden whispered.

She pressed her finger to his lips, silencing him, then took hold of the fabric of her top. She pulled it up and off, and Aiden sighed.

With all they'd been through, all they'd had to endure as a group, this was the first time Aiden could think of where the next moment wouldn't be a battle for survival. This was the first time where he appreciated the moment he was in, and it overjoyed him it was a moment he'd get to share with her. This girl who'd crashed into his life. This girl he'd grown to respect, then admire, then love. This girl who inspired him to live up to his potential. Not because she made him have to, but because she made him want to.

His mystery girl.

"What you said before," Aiden said.

"Before? What you mean?"

"I have a reply," he said as between breaths. "I love you too."

Nemo took his hand, placing it above her breast. Aiden once again experienced her heartbeat.

She leaned back then, pulling him with her.

"Home," she said.

They kissed again, and Aiden loved her. He knew he did; he knew he always had, and he knew he would until the day he died.

The rain let up, its last few droplets making their finale as tiny putters on the metal roof. Aiden and Nemo laid together on an old sofa, as she blissfully played with his hair, her fingers tracing designs only she knew.

She smiled. "I been thinking."

"Oh?"

"When we woke, you see raft anywhere?"

"No. But-"

"Long shot, yes. But we do long shot before."

Aiden nodded. "Worth trying."

Not long after, they had geared up and scavenged what they could from the restaurant. As they exited the building, they both appreciated the new warmth as the sun broke through the exiting rain clouds, and the ocean breeze carried a feeling of stillness they could revel in.

Then they left the pier and headed back into the deserted streets of the abandoned vacation town. As they traveled, she took his hand and squeezed.

The pair searched for their friends, together.

CHAPTER 39

Hobbes and Larina made their way through the lush greenery toward their target. The foliage was thick, and they often had to alter their path or scramble over the plentiful plant life.

"This is amazing," Hobbes said, regarding the surrounding trees. "These plants are so, so-"

"Soft," Larina finished for him.

He turned to find her kneeling in an open grassy patch, running her fingers through it.

"What are you doing down there?" Hobbes asked.

"I've never seen the ground so alive."

"None of us have," Hobbes said as he kneeled next to her. "This place is untouched by the Storm. If we only knew what was out here, just imagine if all the tribes had come with us."

"Are we going back?" Larina asked bluntly. "Are we going back to the Eye to get the others?"

Hobbes thought for a moment, but shook his head. "Not without the Stormwalker. I may be a Pathfinder, but there's no way of knowing where the Eye is now."

Larina nodded. "It's okay. I don't want to go back."

"Neither do I," Hobbes sighed. "I'd rather not think about it until we have to. We made it this far; I think we should get to enjoy paradise for a little while."

Hobbes extended his hand, and Larina took it as he pulled her to her feet.

"I lost my spear," Larina muttered.

Hobbes delivered a slight grin. "Well, let's find you a new one."

They emerged from the brush to find a seemingly endless stretch of road that reached to the horizon behind them. The cracked and crumbling asphalt was littered with the creeping roots of plant life that blurred the line between road and wild.

"Almost there," Hobbes said, pointing ahead. "Look."

Before them stood a group of large structures covered in vines and moss, and beyond them stood the enormous building they had viewed from the beach.

"With any luck we might find some food," Hobbes assured her, and together they hiked ahead on the road until reaching the overgrown complex. As they entered the pavilion, they passed and paused at a large and weathered object. It was a sign, with a white base that rose into a circular shape, with a small white object, like an airplane, flying off and away from the circle. Within the circle sculpted words showed the name of the complex they had arrived at; KENNEDY SPACE CENTER VISITOR COMPLEX.

The two of them, indifferent to the name of the place, continued to the gate. Hobbes tried to slide the doorway to the tourist center open, but it was locked.

"I guess we-" He paused as Larina simply climbed through the glass-less door and disappeared inside. "Or that."

He followed her in. The center was in shambles. Old merchandise littered the floors and shelves. Most items were still in the packaging, some still in good condition even.

As he accidentally stepped on some items, Hobbes leaned over and picked one up.

"No way!"

"What?" Larina asked, concerned. "What did you find?"

"Ice cream!" he exclaimed as he struggled with the foil packaging. "Jonah told stories of this stuff! It was the best thing to eat in the world!"

He finally ripped the package open. He quickly took a large bite of the dehydrated block of food, and it instantly turned to dust in his mouth.

"What's it like?" Larina asked.

Hobbes grimaced as he gave up trying to chew the stuff. "I don't think I like ice cream."

Larina smirked, then noticed something at her feet. She examined it, a writing tool of some kind. It had a message on it; ASTRONAUT PEN: WRITES IN SPACE! She held it out before Hobbes, and he read it as he forced the food down his throat.

"Space," he said. "You know, the black that holds the stars."

"But," Larina pondered, "why would the Stormmakers want to write in space?"

They exited the other side of the center to find an old display area filled with the remnants of space rockets. Some were in pieces, some were fully intact, dozens, maybe hundreds of them filled the area. They were also overgrown with vegetation, having long ago succumbed to nature's claim.

Hobbes climbed atop a toppled-over Saturn 5 rocket. "This is incredible! The Stormmakers *did* travel to the stars!"

Larina sat herself down on a smaller rocket part, unimpressed. "So?"

"So?"

"So what if they could fly? Remember, Nemo could fly, but look where it got her."

Hobbes hopped down to join her. "It's not about that. Look around, look at what they are capable of. *Were* capable of..."

Larina pointed to the distant Storm Wall. "All this stuff didn't help back then. In the Eye, the Thorns had less than any other tribe but survived. And happily. Yet the Eagles and Dogs had everything and look what they became. I'm afraid to become that, Hobbes."

"We won't," Hobbes said. "I promise."

Larina sighed. "Why is this place so empty, anyway? The Storm has never come here."

"Come on," Hobbes stood. "If we find anyone, we'll ask them."

Larina smiled weakly, then took his hand in hers. She leaned closer to him, and they were about to kiss, when the box clipped to Hobbes's belt began to click. They both looked down at it with concern, then noticed the many long shadows forming upon the surrounding ground. They spun around together and faced a group of figures silhouetted by the sun. Then the figures stepped forward.

Marshy swampland surrounded Aiden and Nemo as they hiked down the long road toward the giant building. They each stole the occasional glance at the other, often smiling at each caught the other in a moment.

"Sun setting," Nemo eventually said. "Need shelter soon."

"Shouldn't be much longer," Aiden nodded toward the building. "What do you think that place is?"

Before Nemo could reply, a rustling sound alerted them.

"What was that?" Aiden wondered. "An animal?"

Nemo was quiet, but Aiden couldn't miss the look of fear emerge on her face. Her breathing quickened, and she looked at Aiden, alarmed. "Hurry."

She raced ahead. Without thinking, Aiden followed, but failed to match her pace. Another stretch of marshland moved, and a shape dislodged itself onto the road.

"Go!" Nemo cried.

But it was too late. Aiden turned just as a Stormwalker plowed into him, delivering a swift kick to his chest. Aiden hit the ground but continued on a roll.

"Nemo, run!" Aiden yelled then charged the Stormwalker, fists swinging. The Stormwalker easily dodged, then attacked with a strong palm-strike that knocked Aiden back again. Undeterred, Aiden charged once more. But then a second Stormwalker appeared from nowhere in the marsh and jumped him. The two Stormwalkers restrained Aiden, dragging him to his feet.

But then he realized that Nemo was still there. She hadn't tried to escape at all and was instead walking toward them.

"All right," Nemo spoke solemnly to the two Stormwalkers. "Let's go."

"Nemo?" Aiden tried to ask, but one of the Stormwalkers smacked him over the head.

Then, led by Nemo, the two Stormwalkers dragged the unconscious Aiden away.

CHAPTER 40

The inside of the massive building was extensive. They had refitted machinery into makeshift homes, creating a shanty-town populated by large numbers of robed and ragged figures; men, women and children all.

They led Aiden deeper and deeper into the Stormwalker camp, his head swimming with semi-consciousness over all he saw around him. Groups of Stormwalkers, young and old, watched as they marched past, every one of them wrapped and almost indistinguishable from one another.

They came to a stop. Ahead of them a pair of rocket cones laid across the floor at an angle, making a ramp. Atop one cone emerged a lone Stormwalker. He was larger, his rags and bandages darker, with red trimmings. He also used an ancient elephant gun as a cane. His face, like many of the others, was slightly disfigured, with the lower half adorned with an ashen-gray beard.

Everyone was silent. The Stormwalker studied Aiden. and eventually cleared his throat.

"I see the questions burning in your eyes," the Stormwalker said.

"You... you're all Stormwalkers," Aiden stammered.

The Stormwalker nodded. "We are. I am Obsidian. My apologies, our kind are not used to seeing the face of the Stormmakers. Too clean. Too soft. In your eyes, I see destruction. I see those who started our world, while ending their own."

Aiden was in shock. He tried to speak, but only a weak whimper sounded.

Obsidian continued. "Our skies, once clear and bright, were darkened. Some sought refuge in your Eye. They were trapped, but they were also safe from the poisoned air they'd unleashed. But us, the Storm changed us. Made us anew. Made us evolve. With every generation we left humanity behind."

He nodded at the two Stormwalkers, who released Aiden.

"Are... are you all that's left? Is this all the world outside the Eye?" Aiden asked.

"Few survived the radiation outside the Eye," he replied. "We are those few."

"But why hide? All this time you could have helped us!"

The elder Stormwalker shook his head. "Keeping you in the Eye was the only safety your people had. The only reason you are here now is because the toxic Earth is healing."

"No," Aiden countered, and indicated Nemo who stood ahead of them. "The reason I'm here is because of her."

"Ah," Obsidian acknowledged. "The girl."

"Nemo."

"I know full well who she is!" Obsidian barked. "Question is, do you?"

Aiden was confused, Nemo could tell. She sighed. "You

needed help, Aiden. I couldn't let your people die without giving them a chance."

"Cabhrú thug tú gan mo chead," Obsidian spoke to her in their language. "Anois féach cad tá do ghníomhartha a dhéanamh!"

"Nemo?" Aiden pleaded.

Nemo faced Aiden then and looked directly into his eyes. She could see the love there still, masked behind the fear and confusion. But this would be the real test.

"Aiden," Nemo spoke. "I am a Stormwalker."

He knew. Perhaps he'd known all along, but part of him had ignored the signs. Part of him had to see the mission through, no matter what. Part of him perhaps didn't even care. But still…

"This whole time," he asked, "you were pretending? Lying to us? To me? Why?"

The elder Stormwalker chuckled. "Something we have in common, Aiden, was it?" He descended the ramp and faced Nemo. "How many made it out with you?"

Nemo looked to Aiden, who shook his head. She then faced her elder directly. "Just us."

Obsidian sighed in disappointment. He motioned to a nearby guard, who quickly retreated from the room.

"Only you two," the elder Stormwalker stated. "Really."

Nemo nodded in affirmative while the guard returned, Hobbes and Larina, bound at the wrists, at his side. They placed them next to Aiden.

"Then I guess these two are not part of your mission?" the Stormwalker asked.

Aiden shared a happy, though defeated, look with Hobbes.

They were reunited once again. His instincts had been right. His friends were okay. But for how long?

"But even so," Obsidian continued, "I feel we are missing someone."

Unsure of what the Stormwalker meant, Aiden looked to Nemo for reassurance. But she had none to give.

"You can come out now!" Obsidian suddenly bellowed, his face looking directly above.

Though everyone looked above also, the room remained silent.

"I know you are there, Onyx," the Stormwalker stated. "Come out now. Don't make an old man look foolish."

Still nothing.

Obsidian sighed once more. "Very well."

He lifted his elephant gun to aim on Larina. She took a step back, but a guard shoved her back in place.

Still nothing.

He slowly panned the gun to rest on Hobbes, who clenched his fists in anger.

Still nothing.

Finally, Obsidian brought the gun to bear on Aiden.

Onyx was there in an instant, landing from the shadows above to come between the gun and Aiden. In a flash, Onyx snatched the gun from Obsidian's grasp and spun it around to face its owner.

The room erupted in movement as the other Stormwalkers aimed their firearms at Onyx.

"Onyx," Obsidian smirked. "It has been some time."

Onyx said nothing, choosing instead to maintain his aim on the elder Stormwalker.

"What do you hope to accomplish from all this?" Obsidian asked. "Our worlds are too different."

"Our world is the same," Nemo stated, stepping forward. The guards readied themselves, but Obsidian allowed it. "There are just walls between us, walls the world has created. We are all descended from the Stormmakers. We came from the same place. We cannot keep them in their cage any longer."

"We all agreed they are not ready," Obsidian countered.

"I've seen that they are!" Onyx declared. "You claim we are above them. But I've seen what they have made from so little. I've lived with them. I've fought at their side."

Onyx then lowered the gun, and, in one swift motion, peeled off his face wrappings and goggles.

Aiden couldn't believe what he was seeing. None of them could.

Standing before him was a face Aiden never thought he'd see again; the face of his father.

Aiden stared at the face of Deacon.

CHAPTER 41

Hobbes stared, wide-eyed. "Deacon?"

Deacon paid them no attention. He instead focused on Obsidian. "The fact they are standing here now proves they are capable. Just as much as us."

"Dad?" Aiden spoke, approaching, but Nemo stopped him. She shook her head, but Aiden was awestruck.

"You left us for them," Obsidian stated. "You were a legend to our people. One that inspired. You married into our tribe and proved yourself. The man that not only walked the Storms but tried to unite them. You must know I want to say you were wrong for defying me. For turning your back on your own people. Wrong to drag this girl into your scheme."

Deacon stood defiantly, finally stealing a glance at his son. Aiden nodded, ready.

Obsidian stepped back, letting out a tired breath. "But I can't."

Deacon was surprised, as were Aiden and the others. The room filled with hushed murmurs amidst the Stormwalkers. Nemo, however, cracked a relieved smile.

"You were true to your word to keep the lines of communication open between us and the tribes. And the Eye-dwellers have proven me wrong," Obsidian continued. "To think they made it without our gifts. Onyx, you were right."

"Deacon," Aiden's father replied. "My name is Deacon."

Obsidian relented and finally smiled. The guards then released Larina and Hobbes as the Stormwalkers rose in cheer and celebration.

Aiden and Nemo sat atop the shell of an ancient rocket. They watched as the sun dipped behind the distant Storm.

"This is my first sunset," Aiden realized. "The sun is so clear. Days in the Eye were so short. The sky was so small, but out here..."

Nemo looked at him fondly. "It goes on and on."

He nodded, admiring the orange glow of the setting sun lit upon Nemo's face. He gently stroked her cheek, feeling the warmth of the sun on one side of his fingers, the warmth of her on the other.

"So if you are a Stormwalker, then why-"

"Why does my face look normal?" she finished, smiling. "Not all of us are touched by the clicking air. As the world healed itself, its effects lessened. Eventually we began to be born like you again."

Aiden looked back to the Storm then. "The Eye."

"Do you miss it?"

"No," Aiden admitted. "I just wish more had come with us. I wish more would live."

"Deacon knew it would take a lot to inspire your people," Nemo reasoned. "The mystery of me and the airplane was the best way to convince them."

"To trick them, you mean."

"People don't enjoy being told what to do, Aiden. We knew the only way was if you came to conclusions yourselves. I'm sorry it had to be this way."

"I think I'm starting to understand," Aiden said. "But we lost so much. Only five of us made it. Am I supposed to just forget about all we've lost?"

"You don't forget them," Deacon's voice sounded behind them, and they turned to find him approaching. "You honor them."

"And that's my cue to go," Nemo said as she got up to leave. She took a few steps, but then wheeled around and returned to Aiden.

She delivered a soft kiss on his cheek, pulling away just slightly to whisper in his ear. "Ruby. My name is Ruby."

She grinned, then departed. As she passed Deacon, he patted her shoulder and then sat next to his son.

Aiden touched his cheek and smiled. "You said it was tough being the good guys."

"She is as good as they come around here," Deacon said. "It's hard to impress a Stormwalker, but she's taken a real shine to you."

"So," Aiden struggled to find the right words. "Mom was a Stormwalker."

"She was," Deacon replied, "and I loved her for it. She was an amazing woman, your mother. She inspired me. We wouldn't be here now if it wasn't for her."

"And Jonah?"

"Who do you think helped me disappear?" Deacon revealed. "The body you watched burn was a Dog from an earlier raid. Jonah arranged it all. I really wish he could be here now."

"But why?" Aiden pleaded. "Why put us through all this?"

"Aiden," Deacon struggled. "I was the only one who could lead you through the Storm. But it was you, and you alone, who had to choose whether to go and what you would do. This is what the Stormwalkers are. This is what it means to walk the Storms and live in this world. It's not fair, I know. But sometimes life isn't fair, and that's when your true will is tested. The mission had to be built of real determination if it was to mean anything, to the Eye and the Stormwalkers, and to us."

"But the Stormwalkers tried to stop us!" Aiden argued. "They sent that monster after us."

"Skarn," Deacon agreed. "Skarn was a radical. He believed the people in the Eye had no right to this place. That Eyedwellers were vermin compared to the Stormwalkers. That Stormwalkers were chosen to be the masters of the Storm."

"Jorus and Skarn sound like they were made for each other," Aiden muttered.

"The Stormwalkers did not send him," Deacon reassured. "His actions were his own. Obsidian relented to let Nemo and me try, though he was sure we'd fail. But you proved him wrong. I'm proud of you."

"So what about the others?" Aiden asked. His friends had seen this through with him. No way he would abandon them now. "Can we make a home for them here?"

"They walked the Storm too. They're Stormwalkers, should they choose to be." Deacon stared off into the Storm again, watching the distant arcs of lighting clash and thunder rumble. "Look out there, Aiden. Do you see why the Stormwalkers settled here?"

"It's untouched by the Storm. You're safe here."

"That. But also because of what this place means. This

land was once the height of civilization. The height of mankind's hopes and dreams. The Stormmakers reached for the stars themselves here. But even this place will not remain untouched forever."

More thunder echoed in the sky, but Aiden noticed it coming from another direction. He turned to see the Storm Wall, it's ever-shifting shape and mass traveling the wasteland. But then Aiden realized something, that this Storm Wall was moving in a different direction from the Storm they had escaped.

It was an altogether different Storm.

"Another Storm?" Aiden gasped. "There's more than one?"

"There are many," Deacon replied. "All with their own Eye."

"And where there is an Eye," Aiden finally realized, "there could be people!"

They stood, and Aiden looked out further. There was another Storm Wall, and another, and another. Aiden came to realize they were in the nexus, a point in the world where the many Storms converged and reflected off of each other.

"Within every Eye are things you wouldn't believe," Onyx declared.

To Aiden, the world suddenly seemed much bigger.

"I have something for you," Deacon said as he reached into his tunic. He then withdrew and held the jade ring by its chain, letting it rotate before Aiden.

"But her ring, shouldn't you keep it?" Aiden asked as he watched the ring seem to dance in the light breeze.

"You passed your trials, Aiden. Your mother would be so proud of you," Deacon said. "It's time you took care of it."

Aiden took the ring then and stared at it as it rested in his palm. "So what do we do now?"

"We continue the mission your mother believed in," Deacon said. "The mission I've devoted my life to. We unite the Storms. We make this world livable again."

The wasteland stretched into the vast distance where it met with the gigantic force of the nearest Storm Wall. Obsidian and other Stormwalkers stood at a cliff edge, watching below where Deacon, Aiden, Ruby, Hobbes and Larina were gathered.

The group had equipped in full Stormwalker gear. They congregated around a collection of stone markers, each etched with a different name; Vic, Robin, Bastion, Sparrow, Finch, even Creed.

Aiden spared a glance down at the jade ring looped through the chain around his neck. The ring rested against his chest, and as they walked, he tucked it safely into his vest. There it would be safe, a relic of his mother's legacy, of his connection to the Stormwalker way.

The group regarded the memorial for some time before turning toward the Storm Wall.

"So where's our home gonna be now?" Hobbes joked.

"Home?" Aiden said. He looked to Ruby, the Stormwalker girl who had changed everything for him. The one who pushed him. The one who believed in him. The one he knew he could count on, the one he wanted to be there for. He pulled his goggles on and took her hand in his, their fingers intertwined. "I am home."

They came from different walks of life, but as they headed

into the Storms, they walked together. They would discover what life inhabited those Eyes, and they would work to unite the Storms. Regardless of direction, that was their mission.

If there was to be a future, they had to succeed.

Aiden took notice of the lightning and thunder that seemed to roar their warnings ahead. He recalled his childhood stories then, stories of the thunder that came in the night, thunder that changed the world. They would face that thunder, together.

After all, it all began with the sound of thunder.

THE JOURNEY CONTINUES

Aiden, Nemo, and company continue their adventure in Book 2 of *The Storm Cycle;*

HEART OF THE STORM

Available for order at most booksellers. Get it today to continue the adventure!

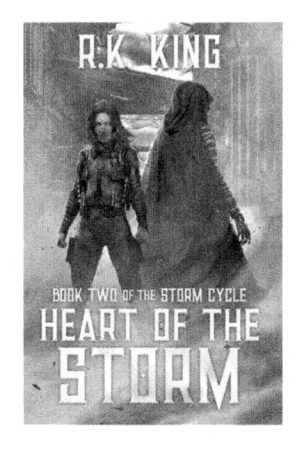

ABOUT THE AUTHOR

R.K. King is a writer of novels, screenplays and short fiction. When not writing or reading, he enjoys movies, video games and generally being a well-rounded nerd. He lives in British Columbia with his wife and cat. Get a FREE short story and keep up to date by joining the RK King readers' list at www.rkkingwrites.com

facebook.com/RKKingWrites
twitter.com/rkkingwrites
instagram.com/rkkingwrites

Made in the USA
Las Vegas, NV
30 November 2020

11754482R00163